A VALENTINE'S KILL

WATERFELL TWEED COZY MYSTERY SERIES: BOOK THREE

MONA MARPLE

For my family, who have cheered my successes and commiserated my losses always.

For my amazing cover designer, Charlie. Thank you for taking my vague ideas and creating such beautiful cover designs!

1

"His Lordship's back, all right." Dorie Slaughter said in between sips of tea. Sandy tried to withhold a smile at the older woman's gossip as she placed a bacon sandwich on the table in front of her and attempted to retreat to the counter.

"Hold on, Sandy, you want to hear this." Elaine Peters said from her seat next to Dorie.

"Oh, I'd love to, I need to finish your breakfast though," Sandy said with a smile, then speed-walked away. Her friend and employee, Bernice, was plating up mushrooms in the kitchen.

"Elaine's?" Sandy asked. Bernice nodded. They didn't get many vegetarians in Books and Bakes and the plate was missing sausage and bacon. "Don't suppose you want to take it out for me?"

Bernice wiped her hands on a tea towel and met Sandy's gaze. "Not a chance, boss."

"Boss?!" Sandy exclaimed.

Bernice laughed. "It's like a witches' coven out there, I'm staying here."

Sandy rolled her eyes but couldn't argue. Everyone who had come to the cafe that morning had been buzzing with the excitement of some new piece of village gossip that Sandy had so far escaped hearing about. She loved Waterfell Tweed, but the villagers were like a swarm of locusts for news and rumours.

"Fine, I'll take one for the team," Sandy said, picking up Elaine's plate and returning to the noisy front-of-house.

"I thought he'd been sacked." Her sister, Coral, called across the cafe from behind the counter. Coral had joined Sandy to work the till when she had been made redundant from her job as a journalist, and she still loved digging for a new story.

"On a sabbatical," Dorie said. "What does that even mean?"

"A sabbatical... well, it's like, erm..." Elaine stumbled over her words. It was unlike Elaine to be involved in village gossip, but Sandy knew she was making an effort to spend more time with Dorie, who had been struggling with loneliness since Elaine began dating her adult son.

"Here you go, Elaine." Sandy said, placing the breakfast in front of her. Elaine grabbed the knife and fork and stabbed a mushroom, then placed it in her mouth and chewed. Her appreciative groans told Sandy she was enjoying the taste.

"Sandy, you'll know..." Dorie called as Sandy turned on her heels to walk away. "What's a sabbatical? Or maybe it was a secondment."

"It's just like a long holiday, isn't it? A few months out away from work?" Sandy said, shrugging her shoulders to show she wasn't sure.

She took a moment to survey the busy cafe and allowed herself a smile. Busy days paid the bills.

As well as Dorie and Elaine, there were at least eight other tables bustling with people, all either tucking into food orders or reviewing the menu.

"It's not funny." Dorie scolded, and it took a moment for Sandy to realise that the woman was speaking to her. Her smile must have been wider than she intended.

"Sorry." Sandy said. She flashed a smile and then walked through the tables to the staircase at the back of the ground floor area, which she walked up into the bookshop area.

Derrick Deves sat behind the counter, still recovering from being run over by a car. He grinned as soon as he saw her. "Come up for a bit of peace?"

"What's got into everyone today?" Sandy asked, then realised that her question made her a gossip talking about gossipers. "Actually, forget I said that. I don't want to know! How's it going up here?"

"Dead easy," Derrick admitted. Sandy had realised before Derrick's injuries that she needed the upstairs till manned full-time, and with Derrick still recovering, he was the perfect person to sit there all day. "I'd rather be up and about, though."

"I know, and you will be soon. I've got a long list of jobs waiting for you." Sandy admitted. They were missing Derrick's pot-washing too, which he had done quicker than anyone else and with a happier heart.

"Glad to hear it. I don't know how people work in offices all day, sitting at a desk... it'd drive me mad."

Sandy shrugged. "You're warm and comfy, I'd take it over being a builder or something where you're outside in all weather."

"Bit of cold killed no one, lady," Derrick said. Sandy raised an eyebrow at him. "Well, yeah, I guess it can actually."

They both laughed until Sandy heard a shriek from downstairs.

Derrick was up off his chair in a shot.

"I'll go, you stay up here and rest your legs." Sandy insisted, placing a hand on his arm. She ran downstairs to see most of the customers peering out of the shop window across the village square. Coral was amongst them, gazing out, and even Bernice had poked her head out of the kitchen. Sandy met her gaze. Bernice shrugged and returned to the kitchen.

"What's going on?" Sandy asked, feeling like a teacher attempting to control an unruly class of children.

Nobody appeared to hear her. If they did, they ignored her.

"What's going on?" She repeated, louder. Coral turned and put a finger to her lips, telling her sister to shush. Sandy rolled her eyes, barged through the crowd, and opened the cafe door. The sun was unusually bright for so early in the year and her eyes struggled to focus for a second in the glare. By the time her sight had adjusted, there was nothing at all to see.

Her cafe stood on one side of the village square, looking out over the small playing field which had a well-ignored 'No Ball Games' sign standing in its middle. As she looked out, the small bus that came through the village twice a day had stopped on the opposite side of the field, and a single man was allowing his Golden Retriever to sniff his way across the field.

"What on earth's got into you lot today?" Sandy asked as she returned to the cafe.

Most of the customers had returned to their tables and several furiously sipped drinks before they cooled.

"Will someone answer me?" Sandy asked, but this question she whispered only to her sister. Her customers came in for many things, but rudeness from the owner wasn't one of them.

"He's here all right. Saw him get off the bus. Dorie got a bit overexcited, you know how she is when she's right."

Sandy definitely knew how Dorie was when she was right - intolerable. Her smugness could last for days.

"Who's here?" Sandy asked.

Coral eyed her, her brow creased with lines she wouldn't want to know were quite so visible. "Dick Jacobs! Haven't you been listening at all this morning?"

"I've been trying not to." Sandy admitted.

"Did you say Dick Jacobs?" Bernice asked, appearing from the kitchen. She smelt of gingerbread and her cheeks had a dusting of flour on them.

"Who's Dick Jacobs?" Sandy asked. She had the distinct feeling that she had been kidnapped by aliens and transported to an alternate reality overnight.

"Is he back?" Bernice asked.

"Dorie came in this morning saying he was, and we've just seen him get off the bus." Coral explained.

"Blimey." Bernice said. "I'd better check our assessments are up-to-date."

"I give up." Sandy said, holding her hands up in defeat.

"All right, Miss Dramatic, what's got into you?" Coral asked, turning her attention to Sandy as Bernice retreated into the kitchen and banged around moving lever-arch files.

"Nothing's got into me!" Sandy exclaimed in a petulant voice that she knew made it obvious something had got into her. "I don't know what any of you are talking about, that's all."

"It's fairly easy." Coral said with a sigh. "Dick Jacobs is back."

"Ah, that settles it then. Why didn't you say?" Sandy said. "Who on earth is Dick Jacobs?"

Silence fell across the cafe and Sandy turned to see most of the customers looking at her with puzzled expressions on their faces.

"You don't know Dick Jacobs?" Dorie asked.

Sandy sighed. She was tired of the whole conversation. "No, I've got no idea who he is."

"I didn't realise his sabbatical had been that long." Gus Sanders said. He was sitting at one of the far tables with his wife, Poppy. "He last came out to me, what must it have been, maybe 2 years ago... nah, must have been longer than that. Wow... time flies."

"It was four years ago, Gus." Poppy said, her voice barely a whisper. "He was against the premises being used as a butcher's, do you remember?"

"He's against everything, that bloke." Gus muttered.

"He's from health and safety, Sandy." Elaine explained.

"Everyone's getting this excited about a health and safety man?" Sandy asked, incredulous.

"He's not a health and safety man, he's the health and safety devil!" Gus said with a snigger. "I think that man dreams at night about the next business he'll close down."

"Surely, it's his job to close down businesses that shouldn't be open?" Sandy said. She couldn't imagine that health and safety officer was a popular job. Probably about as well-liked as traffic wardens. But someone had to do it.

"He'd close everyone down if he could." Dorie said. "Do you remember the wool shop?"

"The Knitting Basket?"

"That's it, thought it might be before your time. He had that place closed down because their kettle was too close to their toilet! And it was only for their own cups of tea, they didn't even serve food or drinks!"

Sandy tried to resist the temptation to roll her eyes. "I can't imagine that's the whole story, Dorie."

"You'll see, you've never been inspected by him before." Dorie said.

"What are you trying to say, Dorie?" Sandy asked, feeling her cheeks flush.

"She's right." Bernice's measured voice came from behind Sandy. Sandy turned to see that her arms were filled with lever-arch files - the records that went into running an establishment that offered food and drink to the public. Temperature checks, food rotation, cleaning records, and more. The records were thorough, accurate and up-to-date, Sandy knew. "Dick Jacobs sees it as his personal mission to close down as many businesses as he can."

Sandy could ignore the customers gossiping, but for the unflappable Bernice to issue such stark words made Sandy shiver as if someone had walked over her grave.

"Can we talk in private?" Bernice asked. Sandy nodded and followed her employee across the cafe area and upstairs to the books.

Derrick was in the middle of serving an elderly gentleman who had been browsing for at least an hour and had an arm-full of books piled on the counter.

"Dick Jacobs is bad news, Sandy." Bernice whispered. She handed the pile of folders across to her. "You need to make sure all of these are in order."

"They are in order, Bernice, we're so careful with them." Sandy said.

"He will find any tiny thing he can, and close us down. He really did close the wool shop, and he's desperate to close Gus' butchers. He's been trying to catch him out for years."

"And he hasn't managed it, doesn't that show we don't need to worry if we're doing things properly anyway, which we are?"

Bernice sighed, her lips pursed. "He has a thing against women in particular, Sandy. When he closed the wool shop down, he told Mabel that she should have been at home cleaning anyway, not trying to run a business."

Sandy felt her cheeks flush. "He really said that?"

Bernice nodded. "He wants to get the butchers closed, but I think he's scared of men. He'll be after you, after us, when he comes. It's his first visit to us, he'll want to find something. Anything."

"Ok." Sandy said. She had never seen Bernice so worried. "Ok, I'll look through these."

"Do it today." Bernice urged.

"I'll do it now." Sandy promised. There was a small office at the back of the upstairs that she never used, but which had a desk and chair left from the previous occupants.

Sandy decided to spend the rest of the morning holed up in the office, making sure that her folders would give Dick Jacobs no excuse to close her beloved business.

2

---

*S*andy jumped at the sound of a light knock on the door which dragged her attention from her work. She stifled a yawn and closed the lever arch folder before calling for the person to enter.

"Sandy, you should come down." Bernice said, her face pale. Her tone of voice told Sandy not to argue. She stood up and followed Bernice out of the room and down the staircase.

The cafe was bustling with people who were, again, gazing out of the window as their food and drinks grew cold.

"What's happened?" Sandy whispered.

Nobody had time to answer her before a bright pink Porsche screeched to a halt outside the cafe and a tall, slender woman in a fur coat jumped out and raced out of sight.

"What's Isabelle doing here?" Sandy asked. Isabelle Irons, owner of the chip shop and various other businesses, was rarely seen in the village and certainly didn't know how to fry fish herself.

"Bad day for businesses and pet owners." A voice came

from behind Sandy. She turned to see Cherry Gentry, the vicar's assistant, leafing through a mystery novel.

"Is it, Cherry?" Sandy asked.

Cherry slammed her book closed and met Sandy's gaze. "I wasn't talking to you."

Sandy felt her cheeks flush and held her hands up in apology, but Cherry had returned to her novel, muttering under her breath as she gazed down at the yellowed pages.

"What are you doing, you awful little man?" The ghost of an Irish accent shouted from outside. Isabelle.

Sandy pulled on her own coat and opened the cafe door, peering to the left to the chip shop, where Isabelle's fur coat was flapping in the wind as she gesticulated wildly towards a man holding a clipboard.

"Is everything okay, Isabelle?" Sandy asked, bracing herself against the weather.

"We don't need an audience, thank you, Ms Shaw." The clipboard man said, although his smug grin suggested he was more than happy to be causing a scene.

"I don't think I know you?" Sandy said, crossing her arms, although she would bet her bookshop that the man was Dick Jacobs.

"You haven't had the formal pleasure yet. That's coming soon. Now, I must get back to my work." The man said as he scribbled notes on his paper. He didn't even give her the courtesy of looking at her.

"Are you ok?" Sandy asked Isabelle in a hushed tone.

Isabelle Irons had looked like a radiant 40 year old for the last 30 years, as far as Sandy could remember. Her true age was anyone's guess.

"He's closing the Fryer." Isabelle said with a lilt.

"What? Why?"

"Because it's my job to close businesses that are a danger

to the public, Ms Shaw. Now I must insist that you leave us alone." The man said, as he finally looked up from his paperwork and gave Sandy a stern look. He stroked his salt-and-pepper moustache as he spoke.

Sandy gave Isabelle a reassuring pat on the arm and walked away reluctantly, back to Books and Bakes. The door was open and Dorie and Cass were both crammed into the doorway watching what was happening.

"I take it that's Dick Jacobs?" Sandy asked as she reached them. Neither moved to allow her back in through the door.

"He's a brave man taking on The Iron Lady." Dorie muttered.

"The Iron Lady?" Cass asked.

"Oh, forget it. You younguns know nothing important."

Cass shrugged and moved aside to let Sandy in.

"Right everyone," Dorie called, closing the door and returning to her usual table. "The Village Fryer has been closed down by health and safety."

While a few customers gasped, most were used to Dorie's outbursts enough to continue what they were doing. Cherry Gentry didn't even look up from her book.

"Dorie, let's leave it until we know for sure what's happening." Sandy urged. While Books and Bakes had been very busy for a while, she had had her fair share of quiet days and cash flow problems. She didn't want to gossip about another business.

"We know what's happening!" Dorie exclaimed. "Dick Jacobs is back and he's starting a war against Waterfell Tweed!"

"A war? Come on, Dorie, we don't need to be so dramatic." Sandy said.

"You'll be dramatic when it happens to you," Cass said.

She had taken a seat next to Olivia, her teenage sister, who looked bored by the whole conversation.

"Olivia, Derrick's upstairs," Sandy said. "If you were wanting to see him."

Olivia broke into a smile and stood up from the table, revealing her bare legs below a denim skirt. She raced up the stairs at the back of the cafe to see her boyfriend.

"Someone's in their hot blood," Dorie said with a disapproving last glance as Olivia disappeared to the upper floor.

"I wore worse at her age and I bet you did too," Cass said with a laugh.

"Anyway, back to the real news," Dorie said. "Dick Jacobs won't stop at the chip shop. Sandy, you need to pay attention to me for once."

Sandy let out a small laugh. "Dorie, I always pay attention to you."

"Did you finish checking the files?" Bernice asked, appearing at the counter to make herself a cup of coffee.

"All done." Sandy confirmed. "And all in order, as I said they would be."

"Good." Bernice said, picking up the fine china cup that she always drank out of and taking a sip. "We need to be on alert."

Sandy shook her head and retreated upstairs to the books. She coughed to announce her arrival, remembering that Olivia was up there to see Derrick. To her surprise, Derrick was at the upstairs counter and Olivia had curled up in a cosy armchair to read a book.

"Are you guys okay?" Sandy asked, looking from one to the other.

"Fine." Olivia said, in that tone of voice reserved for when things are definitely not fine.

Sandy glanced at Derrick, who rolled her eyes. "I told her she shouldn't be out in a skirt like that today."

"Oh... a domestic. I'll leave you to it." Sandy said.

"I don't want a controlling man," Olivia said, and the ridiculousness of those words being spoken by a 15-year-old made Sandy stifle a laugh.

"I'm not controlling you," Derrick said. "It's too cold, that's all I meant and you know it."

"Why don't you take your break now?" Sandy offered. "I'll take over here."

"Yeah, go on then. Thanks, lady." Derrick said, using the palm of his hand on the counter top to help him get to a standing position. "Come on, Livvy, let's get some lunch."

Olivia stood and came to his aid as soon as she saw him struggling. He would make a full recovery from the hit and run, but time was proving to be a slow healer.

"See you later, lovebirds!" Sandy called after them as they made slow progress across to the lift.

Finally, she was alone to enjoy the peace. She busied herself by choosing one of the boxes from the storage room behind the counter and giving all of the stock it contained a wipe with a dry cloth. She had bought the box of second-hand books from a house clearance the weekend before and had been itching to inspect the books within.

Since expanding to take over the first floor as well as the ground floor, she had extended her range of books, meaning that word spread locally and afar, attracting new customers. While the cafe remained a favourite choice with the locals, the bookshop was often full of faces that Sandy didn't recognise.

"Excuse me, dear?" An unsteady voice called from the counter. Sandy emerged from the storage room and placed the book she had been wiping on the counter. An elderly man, his slight weight supported by a walking stick, stood before her, three books in his arms. "Do you buy?"

These requests were increasing. At least three times a day, someone would come into the shop and ask her to buy books they were getting rid of. Most of them came with dog-eared copies of popular fiction, the kind of things that every charity shop had ten copies of, and Sandy would refuse the offer. Occasionally, a person would bring in a collection of more rare and valuable items, and Sandy would be open to discussing a price, although people often imagined everything to be worth a lot more than it actually was.

"No, not usually." She said, but felt a pang of sympathy for the man who had struggled out with his walking stick to offer her his minimal collection. "What are they?"

"Watercolour books." The man said, holding them out for her to see. Sandy gave each title a cursory glance; they all looked in perfect condition. "I meant to start doing it, you know, after Elsie... after... when I was widowed. Never even opened them. I don't want any money, lass, just want them to find a good home."

Sandy took the books from him. "Well, that's a very kind offer. I think I know someone who'd enjoy them, actually. I'll take them, if you'll stay and have lunch on the house."

The man flashed her a smile that reached his watery blue eyes, and nodded his head.

"Come on, I'll help you find a table." Sandy said, leading the man towards the lift at his own pace.

When they reached the metal doors and Sandy pressed the button to call the lift back up, the man let out a small noise. "You've got a lift. I'll be blown."

Sandy turned to him in surprise. "Did you walk up the stairs before?"

"Look at the state I'm in. If I never walked, I'd never be able to walk." He said with a smile.

She stood with the man in the lift and when the doors opened, gestured for him to walk out first. He hobbled across to the seating area.

"Ah, Dorie, just the woman," Sandy called, not surprised to see that Dorie was still in the same seat, drinking a fresh mug of tea. "Can this gentleman take a seat with you?"

Dorie looked up at the man and, to her credit, was out of her seat in a flash to pull one of the other chairs away from the table so he could sit down. "Of course you can, come and have a seat. Dorie Slaughter, pleased to meet you. You've no doubt heard about Jim Slaughter, head of the local constabulary, and yes I am his mum but I really can't talk about his work. Very important, hush-hush, you know."

Sandy made eye contact with Coral, who was standing at the counter serving. The two grinned at each other and rolled their eyes.

"You're about as a subtle as a bull in a china shop." Cherry Gentry muttered. She had almost finished the paperback on her table and, unlike Dorie, hadn't ordered a fresh drink.

The elderly man allowed himself a smile at the commotion as he lowered his frame into the seat. He held out his hand towards Dorie, who offered her own hand in return. Instead of a handshake, he bent his head forward and planted a kiss on her hand, causing Dorie to flush a crimson shade.

"What a pleasure." He said. "Felix Bartholomew, at your service."

"Oh a true gentleman, you can't be from around these parts!" Dorie exclaimed, fanning herself with her hand.

"I'll leave you in Dorie's fine company," Sandy said,

placing a hand on Felix's shoulder. "I'll send Coral over in a few minutes to take your order."

Sandy walked away from the table, weaving in between rows of other tables, all bustling with the lunch-time rush. Coral was busy attempting to work the coffee machine, something she tried and failed at most days.

As much as Sandy dreamed of filling her days in the bookshop upstairs, she was still very much needed in the cafe.

**

Sandy was the last to leave Books and Bakes that night.

The busy day created a mound of dirty dishes that Derrick would have got through in no time, but only being able to scrub a few at a time in between customers made for a long and dirty job at the end of the day.

She had sent Bernice and Coral home when there was nothing but the dishes left to do - with only one sink, it was a job for one person and there was no point having everyone hang around later than needed. But when she finished the dishes, she saw the red and white bunting still waiting to be hung and decided to get that done too.

It was a few days before Valentine's Day, and Sandy had bought the bunting to hang in the window. She stood on one of the chairs to secure the pretty decoration so it hung in a low arc across the window.

As she did a last inspection of the tables and grabbed her coat and scarf, she could hear the strong winds outside. A storm was predicted that evening; a real storm with a name - Storm Selina. It was expected to batter its way across the country and Waterfell Tweed, in its elevated position, would no doubt feel the force of the winds.

Sandy took a deep breath and opened the door. The winds hit her as soon as she was outside, making her scarf slap her across the face as she attempted to lock up. She let out a cry, more surprise than pain, and checked the door handle, then turned to walk across the street where she had left her car.

The village square was deserted, everyone else wise enough to be indoors and warm.

As she walked, she noticed a dark shape on the pavement ahead, and pulled her phone from her handbag, using the torch feature to throw more light on the shape. At first, she thought it was a pile of black bin liners discarded by someone, but as she approached, she realised it was nothing so trivial and she stiffened.

She switched the light off her phone and dialled 999.

"Hello? I need to report a crime - a man has been killed." She said, her voice almost drowned out by the howling winds. As she spoke, she turned her back on the shape on the pavement. The dark pool spooling out from his head told her that Dick Jacobs had shut down his last business.

3

"Can you manage without me tomorrow?" Sandy asked as soon as Coral opened her front door.

Her sister looked at her and stifled a yawn. "Nice to see you too. Are you coming in?"

She propped the door open, and Sandy dove inside out of the wind. Coral gazed at her more closely then and must have noticed how her whole body was shivering with more than just cold.

"What is it? What's happened?" She asked.

"Dick Jacobs has been killed." Sandy said, collapsing onto one of the high stools in Coral's kitchen.

"No way? Wow... I didn't see that coming." Coral said as she filled the kettle with fresh water. "How do you know?"

Sandy felt a lump catch in her throat and cried as she admitted, "I found him."

The big mug reserved for Sandy's visits fell straight out of Coral's hand and hit the floor, smashing into pieces across the tiles.

"Damn." Coral cursed under her breath, then grabbed a small dustpan and brush and swept the pieces into the metal bin, where they clattered as she dropped them in. "Let me try that again."

She fetched another, smaller, cup out of the cupboard and poured Sandy a hot, frothy mocha. She always had a few sachets in for her sister's visits. Coral placed the steaming hot drink in front of Sandy, who smiled her thanks.

"So why do you need us to manage without you tomorrow?" Coral asked, setting a black coffee in front of her own stool and sitting down beside Sandy.

"I want to speak to Isabelle." Sandy said, with a shrug. "See what she knows."

"You mean you want to investigate?" Coral asked with a groan. "Can't you just leave it to the police, Sand? I don't want you getting involved in this."

"I'm already involved," Sandy said, wiping her eyes. "As awful as everyone says Dick Jacobs was, I'm sure he didn't deserve to be killed. And I think I'm good at this stuff, I think I can work it out."

"That man must have more enemies than I've had hot dinners!" Coral said.

"That's why I need to speak to people, and I need you to keep your ear out in the cafe tomorrow. See what people are saying."

Coral sighed. "Okay."

"Thanks, sis."

"Want to sleep here tonight?" Coral offered.

Sandy nodded. "Yes, please."

"I'll go and make up the spare bed." She said, and gave Sandy's shoulder a squeeze. Then she stood up and padded through the kitchen and into the hallway before Sandy heard her soft footsteps climb the stairs.

Sandy sat for a while, nursing the hot cup in her hands,

aware of every noise that Coral's house made. Her water pipes gurgled and her heating system hummed as if the house was determined to remind them that it was old despite Coral's modern transformation of its interior.

After a while she pulled out a notebook and pen from her handbag and wrote in the middle of a page: 'Dick Jacobs'.

Next to his name she scrawled 'Isabelle Irons' and then, out of ideas and feeling nervous of being alone, left her drink and joined her sister upstairs.

**

When Sandy awoke the next morning, she had a brief few moments of forgetting what had happened the day before, and then she felt the heaviness in her stomach - dread - and remembered what she had seen.

She glanced across at the small clock that sat on the bedside table and groaned. It was after 10am.

She couldn't remember the last time she had slept so late and yet she still felt tired right through to her bones.

After a quick shower, Sandy searched Coral's kitchen cupboards for something easy for breakfast. She checked behind packets of spelt and barley, squeezed an avocado harder than she should have when picking it up, and turned her nose up at the almond milk in the door of the fridge. Coral's kitchen was a blend of every nutritional fad to hit the headlines in the last 12 months, which was ironic given how much she lived on black coffee and bacon at the cafe. Finally, Sandy grabbed an individual carton of orange juice and an apple, and left the cottage, locking the door behind her.

It was a bright day, the sun sitting high in the cloudless sky, and Sandy put on her sunglasses before starting the car.

Her first mission was to find Isabelle Irons - before the police did.

**

While Isabelle Irons drove a nice car and owned several businesses, she was strapped for cash. She'd lived in the same terraced house for as long as Sandy had known her. Every man-friend she had had in that time moved in with her, and then left quietly at some point later, their name never to be mentioned again. There had been an Arthur, a Cedric, an awkward spell of three Angus' in a row (how was it even possible to find three Angus' in a row?!), a Patrick and a Malcolm. It was as if Isabelle's only criteria for picking a temporary mate was that their name absolutely must be old-fashioned.

As Sandy approached on foot after parking her car out of sight, she could see Isabelle's pink Porsche. The private plate hid the age of the vehicle and as Sandy walked along the pavement she could see that the inside of the car was not as plush as she may have expected. The leather seats were worn, splitting in some places and sagging in others (thanks to the second Angus, no doubt, who was a rather portly passenger), and the passenger footwell was over-flowing with a mound of paperwork, empty water bottles and cuddly toys.

Forcing her eyes away from the chaos of Isabelle's car,

Sandy walked up the small path and knocked on the front door. She had been inside Isabelle's home once, for a reason she could no longer remember, and found it to be as well-presented and ageless as its owner. Her style for interior design was either on the cutting edge of the highest fashions or so old-fashioned that it had become in vogue for the second time around.

Quiet footsteps inside were audible straight away, and Sandy braced herself. She had become involved in murder cases before, but this would be her first time actively attempting to solve the case right away.

Isabelle opened the door wide in a leopard-print silk gown that hung open, revealing a matching camisole. Her feet were bare, her long toenails painted in the same electric pink shade as her car. She had a full face of make-up on and her hair sat on top of her head in that effortless style that was almost impossible for Sandy to perfect.

"Sandy, what a delight," Isabelle said, making no move to allow her to enter.

"Isabelle, I need to talk to you. Can I come in?" Sandy asked.

Isabelle shrugged and stood to one side. Sandy entered and felt her senses reach overwhelm from all of the different patterns, colours and textures on display.

"Let's sit in the front." Isabelle said, gesturing to the first door off the corridor. The terraced houses had all originally had a front room and a back room downstairs. Lots of the new owners had either knocked the wall through to make one large living area, or joined the back room with the original tiny galley kitchen to make a bigger space. Isabelle's home was one of the few still with the original layout, and Sandy found it comforting. She remembered playing with friends from school who lived in houses like Isabelle's, and how the parents would sit in whichever room was left for best, while the kids took over the other.

Isabelle's front room had a feature wall of pink flamingos, flanked on all sides by walls of silver glitter paper. It most certainly wasn't that way the last time Sandy had visited.

"What an amazing space!" Sandy gushed because one could hardly walk in to flamingos and glitter without complimenting it.

"I suppose you're not here to talk about Malcolm's decorating skills." Isabelle said, and Sandy realised. Every man must have changed the house when they arrived. Maybe she got rid of the man when she tired of the decorating, Sandy mused. "I'm guessing you're here to talk about Dick Jacobs being killed. Not tell me about it, hopefully, because I already know."

"I don't know if you know," Sandy began. She fidgeted as she spoke. Being so open about her credentials wasn't Sandy's style. "But I've solved the murders we've had in the village, and I've seen the city police turn up and make a mess of things. I don't want that to happen again."

"And you think they're going to pounce on me as their prime suspect?" Isabelle asked.

"Yes, I do." Sandy said, quietly, as if she was breaking bad news.

Then, to her surprise, Isabelle laughed. "I'm ready for their visit, dear. And trust me, there's an awful long line of people with a grudge against that man. Bigger grudges than I could have had... I could tell you three people right now who would have more of a reason to end his days than I did."

"But, he... he just closed your business that day." Sandy said.

"One of my businesses. And not a profitable one. To be honest, I'd be happy to see the back of the place - there's no money in fish and chips."

"Isabelle, you don't have to be brave with me, I heard you with Dick Jacobs. I heard how devastated you were."

Isabelle shrugged. "Look, I want to be in control of my life, and if I decide there's no money in fish and chips, I want to shut the place on my own terms. I was angry - furious - with that pathetic little twerp, because how dare he! You heard anger, nothing else."

Sandy sighed and took a seat on one of the floral patterned settees, without being invited to. "You're still the most obvious suspect."

"Don't you want to know, then?" Isabelle asked, gazing straight at her.

"Want to know what?"

"Whether I did it, of course!"

4

*A*fter the disaster that had been her first active interview in her unofficial investigation, Sandy woke on Wednesday morning with the echo of a headache still throbbing through her temples. Her alarm seemed to screech at her without mercy, every shrill tone sounding out with glee. In defeat, she reached an arm out from the cosy bed covers and slammed the top of the alarm, hearing part of the intricate mechanics twang ominously.

"Urgh." She groaned as she pulled herself to a sitting position and forced her eyes to open. She always slept with the curtains open, but there was no light to pour in at such an early time on an early February morning. She picked up her phone which was charging at the side of the bed, saw she had received no messages, and felt her stomach churn again. If she didn't own Books and Bakes, she might have considered ringing in sick. Taking what she had heard the Americans called 'a mental health day'.

It felt very much that in recent months, Sandy's life had strayed from the comfort of baking and selling books into a much more risky territory.

She dragged her tired body into the bathroom and took a long, hot bath, keeping her hair out of the water so she wouldn't have to fuss with washing and drying it. After washing her body, she picked up the mystery book she had started a few days before and allowed herself to replace her own worries with those in the story. Reading always soothed her. It had done when her mother had died years before, and during every crisis since.

**

"What time do you call this?" Coral called as Sandy walked into the cafe kitchen, where Bernice was taking a selection of freshly baked cakes from the oven. Sandy raised an eyebrow at her sister but said nothing.

"Smells good." She said instead, directing the comment to Bernice.

"Rocky road," Bernice said and pulled a face towards the chocolate and marshmallow creations. "Too sweet for me."

"A baker who doesn't like sweet things, how novel," Coral said. She was in a mood.

"What's got into you?" Sandy asked.

"She's sulking because her Mr. Right turned out to already have a Mrs. Right." Bernice said in her matter of fact way.

"Who's Mr. Right?" Sandy asked, but Coral shook her head and moved towards the doorway that separated the kitchen from the shop.

"Nobody." She muttered as she left.

Sandy glanced at Bernice, who rarely got involved in anybody's personal drama.

"She's internet dating again," Bernice said, her lips pursed. "I've warned her, but you know what she's like."

"Oh no," Sandy said under her breath. "Not again. I thought she'd learned after the last guy."

"In her defence, she knows there aren't that many eligible bachelors in Waterfell Tweed... especially since you've got your claws into the most eligible one of all."

The idea of Sandy having claws in any man would have made her smile at any other time, but instead, her cheeks flushed and her eyes watered.

"Oh no, I'm sorry. I didn't mean to pry. This is why I stay out of things - normally - but I just couldn't stand by and see Coral get hurt again. It's not my business, Sandy, I'm sorry I made light of it." Bernice said, gabbling away in a frantic attempt to undo whatever wrong she had done.

"It's fine, Bernice, it's not you," Sandy said, gulping back the tears that threatened to escape. "The truth is, I haven't heard from Tom Nelson in a while. We were never officially anything more than friends, and I feel like a fool to have misjudged it so badly."

Bernice gave her a sad smile. "You should pop over to The Tweed and ask him what's what."

Sandy snorted a laugh through her nose. "I don't think I'll ever show my face in there again."

"Oh, Sand." Bernice said, giving her arm a supportive rub. "It'll be ok, whatever happens."

Sandy wanted to say she knew that, that she just felt silly for embarrassing herself, that she didn't even know Tom Nelson enough to have any feelings other than embarrassment at a misunderstanding, but she said none of that. She just smiled at Bernice, nodded, and joined Coral in the shop.

The cafe was completely empty. Derrick was upstairs

manning the bookshop till and Coral was managing to look busy despite having nothing at all to do until a customer arrived.

"What time is it?" Sandy asked.

Coral glanced at her phone, sat on the counter beside the till. "Ten to nine."

"Has nobody been in yet?" Sandy asked. The cafe had been open twenty minutes.

Coral shook her head.

"Strange."

"How did it go with Isabelle?" Coral asked, the quietness giving an excuse for them to chat more than they ever usually did at work.

"Not well," Sandy said, folding her arms across her chest. "Isabelle Irons is a strange woman. I went across there convinced she was innocent, and by the time I left she'd made me suspect her!"

Coral frowned. "Really? How did she manage that?"

"Well, she almost dared me to ask her outright if she'd done it, and when I did, she didn't deny it."

"That's really weird. Why would you want to be encouraging people to think you've killed someone? Whether you have or not? Is she right in the head?"

"Coral!" Sandy scolded, although similar thoughts had run through her own mind, just more politely phrased. The conversation was halted then as the cafe door opened and the day's first customer walked in.

"Morning, Sebastian." Sandy called. Sebastian Harlow had recently returned to Waterfell Tweed after travelling the world. His parents, Penelope and Benedict, were still keeping a low profile, but Sebastian popped in the cafe most days, usually to grab a strong black coffee to go.

"Good morning! How are my favourite ladies?" He

crooned, striding across to a table with the air of a person who felt entirely comfortable in their own skin. Sebastian was young, early 20s, and handsome in a way that was mainly related to the perfect bone structure his face enjoyed. He was immensely good fun and Sandy liked him a lot.

"Better now you're here, Romeo. What do you fancy?" Coral asked, calling across to take his order from the counter.

"Ah, stay back, play it cool... I like your style." Sebastian teased, then glanced at Sandy. "She's more feisty than you, this one."

"She's more feisty than most." Sandy said, winking at her sister.

"I'll have whatever you think I'd like most, and when I say that, I mean the full English of course." Sebastian said. "You should know how I take my coffee since we're practically married."

"When we marry I'll be enjoying the good life. My coffee making days will be over." Coral said with a laugh. Sebastian was due to inherit Waterfell Manor, the grand stately home that had been in the Harlow family for generations. His future wife would indeed enjoy the good life, but that wife wouldn't be Coral.

"I'll massage your feet while the staff make coffee." Sebastian said, then erupted into a raucous laugh. "Geeze, my chat up lines are awful. No wonder I've been single for weeks."

"Weeks?!" Coral and Sandy both repeated in unison.

Sebastian shrugged. "Months, maybe. But that's between us, I have a reputation to maintain."

Sandy rolled her eyes and took the food order back through to the kitchen for Bernice to prepare.

"You ok?" Bernice asked, looking up from the fridge, where she was checking stock levels.

"Yeah, I'm good, honestly. And we've got the village joker in, that's always a laugh." Sandy said. She flashed Bernice a winning smile and pinned the order to the front of the empty queue, then returned to the shop. Coral's face was pale and even Sebastian had stopped talking.

"What's wrong?"

"There's someone here to see you, in private. He's upstairs." Coral whispered.

Sandy let out a sigh and trudged through the cafe, climbing the staircase at the back of the shop as slow as she could. She had no idea what Tom Nelson might want to say to her in private. Perhaps he'd want to apologise for the sudden change, how he transformed so quickly from inviting her on apparent romantic days out to not even sending as much as a text message for almost a week. Maybe he'd be angry, because as much as he had gone quiet, her pride hadn't allowed her to chase him for contact. Or maybe he was in her beloved bookshop upstairs to tell her she had only ever been a friend, that he had backed off because she had grown too attached to him, or even that he had begun a relationship with someone else.

Her stomach flipped with nerves as she made the slow climb upstairs.

So set was she on seeing Tom Nelson, that her eyes failed to recognise anyone else upstairs. She walked the length of the store, peering down every row of bookcases, until a voice called her name from behind.

She turned, and standing before her was her visitor.

"DC Sullivan?" She asked, the dread in her stomach rushing out of her body and then immediately returning. The city police officer stood around 20 feet away from her, in his regular clothes. Dark jeans, a black polo shirt, running shoes.

"We meet again." He said, with a smile that was not unpleasant. "Can we talk?"

"Of course," Sandy said, glancing behind her towards the till, where Derrick sat reading a book. His mobility was so limited still, there was little he could do other than sit and serve, so Sandy had told him to bring a book with him and read when there were no customers. "There's an office up here, follow me."

She lead DC Sullivan to the small office where she had reviewed all of the cafe's records just two days ago, before she had found Dick Jacobs' body. She gestured for him to take one of the two seats and closed the door behind them.

"I guess this is about…"

"Sandy, this isn't an easy visit for me to make." He said, speaking over her. "I've had a complaint about you."

"What? You're kidding?" She said, feeling the colour drain from her face.

"No. No, I'm not. I'm hoping an informal warning will be enough to deal with this, because if it isn't, I come back in my uniform and take you to the station in a patrol car."

"I know the procedure." Sandy said, her voice so quiet she wasn't sure if she had actually spoken.

"Isabelle Irons has reported that you visited her yesterday and accused her of killing Dick Jacobs."

"Well, I - I - I…"

"I know you have this weird interest in the cases happening here, and I've tried to tell you before to back off, but you can't go around accusing people of murder." DC Sullivan said. He closed his eyes and rubbed his temple. "If she isn't the murderer, then you've offended her, and if she is the murderer, you've put yourself in danger."

Sandy gulped. She had been so sure of Isabelle's innocence before her visit that she had been sure the visit would have been about gathering evidence to help clear her name. She had expected Isabelle's gratitude. But calling the police, putting the thought in their mind that she was being considered a murder suspect... Sandy couldn't decide if that idea was stupid or genius.

"I need you to leave this well alone." DC Sullivan said, his voice firm but dog-tired. "Can you promise me that?"

Sandy took a deep breath and crossed her fingers beneath the table, then met the officer's gaze, and nodded.

5

*D*orie waltzed into Books and Bakes at 1.15pm, her beaming smile begging anyone to ask her where she had been all morning. The last time she had been absent from the cafe for a whole morning, it was because she was in hospital with pneumonia.

Sandy watched her, while fighting between pretending to not have noticed she had walked in and guilt she hadn't checked up on her earlier to see if she was okay.

Bernice raised a perfectly arched eyebrow at Sandy on her way back into the kitchen, but said nothing.

It was Coral who gave in. Coral who still had the nose for a story.

"What's got into you today, Mrs. Slaughter?" Coral called across the cafe as Dorie took a seat at an empty table. The cafe was in the middle of the lunch rush, and several people looked up from their own business to see why Coral was calling across the room. She was so used to working in an open plan office, where privacy had no value. Sandy had been meaning to talk to her about it.

"I didn't realise I had to tell you my whereabouts," Dorie said, with a theatric grin on her face.

"Shh!" Cherry Gentry said, raising her face from another mystery novel she had been devouring on her lunch break from the church. For such an avid reader, she'd never bought a book from Books and Bakes.

"Oh shush yourself," Dorie replied, waving her hand in Cherry's direction.

"Tell me to shush myself, they will," Cherry mumbled to herself.

"Come on then, Dorie, where have you been? We all know you're dying to tell us." Gus Sanders shouted from his own table, where he was enjoying a bacon sandwich smothered in red sauce.

"Got a gentleman friend," Cherry said, not taking her eyes off her book. It was impossible to say whether she was talking to anyone but herself or about anyone but herself, but Dorie's cheeks flushed all the same.

"Ridiculous!" She said, with an awkward laugh. "I allowed the gentleman to share my table. A good deed - Sandy, you insisted on it."

Sandy nodded. "That's right, I did. Felix was a bit of an old fox, wasn't he, actually?"

"He was a very pleasant man, but my tardiness today certainly isn't because of having my head turned by an octogenarian," Dorie said. "Get me a pot of tea, Sandy, and a sausage roll."

"Coming right up," Sandy said, pleased for an excuse to turn her back on the inane conversation. The villagers were like rabid animals sometimes, desperate for their next slice of gossip or joint of news.

"Come on then, Dorie..." Coral pushed, oblivious to Sandy's frustrations.

"Fine, if you must know, I was moving house," Dorie admitted.

Sandy turned on her heels. She had hoped that her suspicions that Dorie wanted to leave the village and move to an assisted living residence were wrong. Her stomach sank at the news. Dorie wasn't only the cafe's most loyal customer, she was a comforting face to have around so much.

"You're moving?" Sandy croaked, the upset visible in her voice.

"Well, she won't give her cottage up, so if Mohammed won't come to the mountain, the mountain'll have to go to Mohammed... that's what they say, isn't it?"

"Mohammed? What are you talking about?" Gus asked, less patient than some of the villagers, and since his wife had insisted he cut down his drinking, he'd been ready to snap at most people with little provocation needed.

"Me and Jim are moving in with Elaine." Dorie said as she rolled her eyes towards Gus.

Coral stifled a gasp and Sandy poked her in the ribs.

"All three of you in Elaine's little cottage?" Coral said as she composed herself. "How..."

"How lovely," Sandy said, realising that the news meant that Dorie was her new next door neighbour. "What an exciting change."

"Well, my Jim couldn't leave either of us alone at night with all these murders happening," Dorie said, her tone serious suddenly. "I used to think Waterfell Tweed was the safest place on Earth."

"What are you going to do with your house?" Cherry asked, saving her page with her finger while she looked up. She didn't look at Dorie but gazed into the distance somewhere near her.

"Don't you get any ideas, I wouldn't let you and your cats over the front doorstep," Dorie said.

Cherry stood up, pushing her chair backward with such force it screeched its way across the floor, making an awful noise. She folded the corner of the page she was reading and placed the book in her handbag, then returned her gaze towards but not on Dorie, shook her head, and stormed across the cafe.

"Not the cats she should worry about," Cherry muttered under her breath as she left.

Sandy sighed and walked into the kitchen. Bernice gazed up at her from the sink, where she was attempting to keep on top of the growing pile of dirty dishes. "What's up?"

"Do you think people get nasty towards each other when there's a murder?" Sandy asked.

Bernice let out a small laugh. "Absolutely. It's why I stay in here. People either want to gossip about things they don't know or fight with people they don't like. It's as if all the tolerance they have goes out the window."

"I guess it's that feeling of knowing someone amongst us has done something awful," Sandy said. "Nobody knows who to trust."

Bernice placed another plate to dry. "Are you still determined to get involved in it all?"

"I have to, Bernice. DC Sullivan doesn't care about this place, and these people, like I do. I know I can work out who the killer was."

"Who are your suspects then?" Bernice asked.

"Well, I didn't think it was Isabelle Irons but her behaviour's been very strange, so I don't think I can rule her out now."

"Her behaviour's always strange," Bernice said, and

Sandy remembered that Bernice worked for her, pulling shifts there when Books and Bakes was quiet.

"How?"

"I'm not going to gossip about her," Bernice said.

"I'm not asking you to. This isn't gossip, it's for my investigation. Tell me whatever you think's relevant."

"I have no idea what's relevant, Sandy. I'm happy hiding in here and keeping myself to myself. All I'm saying is, Isabelle has always been odd. Her behaviour's unpredictable. I've heard rumours she's on medication but she doesn't take it all the time. You know how she owns so many businesses but doesn't have two bob to rub together? And how the men come and go? People say she's got some kind of personality thing, like a disorder, and when she has a bad spell she spends the money and kicks the men out. But I don't know if any of that's true."

"So what do you know about her?"

Bernice shook her head. "That's the thing, I know nothing about her. She's never at the chip shop. She's not a hands-on boss like you and you know what people are like; nobody likes to think they're cleaning floors every night for a boss who can't even show her face and say thank you as if the wages she pays aren't enough. I have no idea what kind of person she is."

"There are so many mysterious people in this village," Sandy muttered.

"There are mysterious people everywhere," Bernice said with a smile. "Who else is on your suspect list?"

"I guess Gus Sanders should be... someone said Dick Jacobs was trying to shut his butchers down."

Bernice wrinkled her nose. "Nah, he's tried for years and got nowhere with it. I think Gus thought that man was a joke."

"Who else could want him dead?" Sandy asked, at a loss for ideas.

"If you're struggling with who, move to a different question. Do you know how he died?"

"Ah!" Sandy said, her mind returning to the night she had discovered Dick Jacobs' body. "I'm not an expert but I think I've seen enough detective shows to say it was a blow to the head."

"Ok, well there's your starting point," Bernice said, and Sandy felt her attention return to the dirty dishes. She wondered if she was one of those bosses who didn't get their hands dirty, like Isabelle not cleaning the floors of the chip shop, but she had a murder investigation to solve.

"That's brilliant, thank you, Bernice, you're a star," Sandy said. And then, feeling self-conscious about the fact she had stood around chatting for five minutes, added. "I think that's my lunch break over, I'll get back upstairs."

She left Bernice and walked across the length of the cafe, then climbed the staircase to the first floor. Derrick was at the counter, scrolling through images on his phone.

"Go on, get your lunch, the cavalry's here!" Sandy exclaimed, her presence beside him making him jump.

"Thanks, lady." He said with a coy smile.

"What are you up to? You were concentrating hard on something." Sandy teased.

He held his phone up and she saw he had been looking through photos of the nearest college. An image of its old red-brick facade filled his screen.

"Wow." She said. "You thinking of applying?"

He shrugged, shy. "I dunno, it's just a mad idea. I'd still work here, if you'd have me, just thinking I should try and get some qualifications under my belt. Dad always said nobody can take your education away from ya. They do bricklayin' and all sorts, I could learn a trade."

Sandy looked at him and beamed with pride. "I think it's an excellent idea. Why don't you see when the next open day is and have a look around?"

"Yeah... yeah... I might do. Thanks, lady." Derrick said, his cheeks flushing. He stood up from the chair and Sandy noticed that his movements were a little quicker, smoother, and his body didn't contort into as much pain as it had a week earlier. She watched him walk across to the lift, then took his place on the seat and allowed her thoughts to unravel.

Dick Jacobs had been killed by a blow to the head.

She'd bet her life on it if that wasn't a little insensitive.

That meant that the assailant had been very close to him when he was attacked.

Sandy searched her memory and wished she had been brave enough to have inspected his lifeless body that night. She could picture the shape of him, his hands sprawled out at either side of his body as if he had toppled down as he stood.

"Oh no." She murmured.

He *had* toppled down as he stood. His hands had been unmarked.

He hadn't had the chance to protect himself.

He hadn't seen it coming.

6

*S*andy spent the rest of the afternoon upstairs in the bookshop. She had boxes of new stock to check, price and add to the shop's new inventory catalogue. When the books had taken over only a small portion of the downstairs area, she hadn't bothered using any system to track which books she had. The time and cost to set a system like that up weren't worthwhile for such a small selection. Instead, customers had to rifle through the stock and grab whatever took their fancy.

When she had taken over the upstairs, setting up an inventory catalogue had been on her list of jobs to do. It would allow her to check instantly whether they had a particular book, and would boost sales.

She had been spending some time each day adding the existing stock to the system, and it had been an enjoyable job. She got to walk around each aisle, in turn, selecting each book and scanning it on the hand-held device she had bought. It was the kind of job she had dreamed of doing when owning a bookshop was her biggest wish.

"Sandy?" Derrick's voice called from the end of the

aisle, where she was adding military books to their shelf after scanning them. The distraction from her thoughts made her jump. The bookshop's lights were on and the sky outside had grown a deep blue as it approached pitch black.

"Ooh! Sorry, Derrick, everything ok?" She asked.

"Yeah, I just didn't want to leave you on your own." He said. "It's after 6."

Sandy laughed. "Really?! Oops! I guess downstairs has gone a bit quiet... have they all closed up?"

"Yeah, I told Bernice I'd stay with you but that was at quarter past five. I wouldn't mind but I've got to meet Olivia, I don't want to let her down."

"Oh, Derrick, you go, honestly. I've nearly done here, the time must have got away from me. Just lock me in on your way out?"

"Yeah, if you're sure."

She nodded and he held up his hand in farewell.

Sandy had four books left to add to the military section, a popular area of stock that she was always ready to extend with good quality books. She stood back when she had finished and admired her handiwork. There was something rewarding about seeing the books lined up so neat, in size and subject order. She gave a nod and returned to the small room used for holding new stock.

The room was bare, with three boxes waiting to be added to the inventory and the shelves, and a small table and chair against the wall. As Sandy was about to close the door, she noticed books on the table and wondered if she had forgotten them from the military books she'd just been working with.

A closer look revealed them to be the watercolour books that she had bought from the elderly man. She had hoped that Rob Fields would have been in the shop so she could offer them to him, but she hadn't seen him.

With nothing better to do with her evening, she walked the books across to the church to see if Rob was there.

She picked up the books, went downstairs and put on her coat and scarf, and then turned off the lights and locked up. It was a cool evening but there was no wind, which was rare for Waterfell Tweed in the winter, and the village green was empty apart from a woman walking a large dog. The woman waved and Sandy waved back, thinking it was probably Elaine Peters and her Dalmatian Scamp, but not being sure.

Sandy walked across the green instead of the pavement, averting her eyes from the spot where she could remember Dick Jacobs lying. The church was just off the main square itself, next to Gus Sanders' butchers. She could see that lights were on as she approached, and let herself in the grand wooden door at the front.

"Rob?" She called as she entered and saw that it was empty inside. Sandy was not a religious woman but standing in a church, even a small church like this one, was a humbling experience for her. She also found it slightly unsettling and didn't want to stay too long.

Having only visited Rob Fields at the church a few times, usually to drop off leftover foods for his regular soup kitchen, Sandy knew that the church offices used by him and Cherry Gentry, who was his assistant, were down a corridor to the left of the main chapel.

Keeping an eye on the life-size Jesus on the cross that hung on the wall behind the pulpit, she followed the small corridor. She could see the door to Cherry's room and knew that from that room, there was a door to the vicar's private area, which then had a separate door back into the main chapel. The building was small but the space was used so well, once inside it felt almost cavernous.

"Got to get the salmon, sweetheart." Cherry Gentry's voice sang out from behind the half-open door, making Sandy stop in her tracks. Cherry Gentry had been single for as long as Sandy had known her. She'd always believed that the woman's love was only focused on the hoards of cats she owned. Sandy didn't want to intrude on a personal conversation, and found herself with no choice instead but to loiter around in the corridor until enough time had passed.

"I'll get it," Cherry muttered after a few seconds of silence. A phone call, Sandy thought, a domestic about who picked up dinner. The thought made her mind return to Tom and his silence, and how easily she had allowed herself to picture the possibilities for their future.

She sighed and pushed open the door with a false confidence, as though she had no idea that someone was in there.

Cherry was sitting at a small computer desk, the type that people had years ago, with the built-in lower shelf for a printer and side shelf for the tower, with a keyboard shelf underneath the desk counter. There was no computer or printer in sight. Instead, Cherry had an A4 page-a-day diary spread open to a page where the white of the paper was barely visible beneath the scrawled notes in at least five colours, and next to it, a dog-eared mystery novel with an old receipt sticking out of a page to mark her place.

She was sitting gazing at the diary and turned to look at Sandy with a level of disinterest that would suggest she was always popping in and disturbing her work - although what work that was, Sandy had no idea. She was definitely not on the phone with anyone.

"Cherry, hi, good to see you. Is Rob about?" Sandy asked.

Cherry shook her head. "Home visit. I'm finished now too, got to get the salmon, so you'll have to go"

"Oh," Sandy said, holding up the books she had brought over. "Rob asked me to keep my eyes out for watercolour books, I wanted to show him these."

"I've told her he's not here," Cherry said to herself and then as if she hadn't just spoken out loud, repeated for Sandy's benefit. "I've told you he's not here."

"Ok. Maybe you could ask him to pop over to the bookshop?"

"Maybe." Cherry shrugged and stood up from her computerless computer desk. She was already in her coat and scarf and Sandy wondered if she wore them all day - it was cold enough to need to inside the church. "See if I remember."

"Shall we walk out together?" Sandy suggested as they were both stood up and ready to leave. The request made Cherry flush crimson.

"I'm only going to the butcher's," Cherry said with the panic of a deer in the headlights. "Got to get my salmon."

"Of course," Sandy said. "You mentioned. Is it a special dinner?"

"Eh?' Cherry asked, screwing her nose up in confusion. "No, I always get salmon for my babies."

"Lucky them!" Sandy exclaimed, backing out of the room. "I'll see myself out."

Cherry offered no farewell, and Sandy retreated down the corridor, almost colliding with Rob Fields as he walked back into the chapel.

"Sandy!" He said, with a smile, noticing the books tucked into her side. "You look like Cherry, walking around with a book! Every time I poke my nose through to ask her something, she's reading."

"Busy job, then?" Sandy quipped.

"Ha! Well, no... not busy at all. She likes it though, I think. Gives her time to herself. Are you here for time to yourself?"

"Oh no, I came to see you, actually," Sandy said.

"Got to get the salmon, in a rush!" Cherry muttered as she walked past the two of them and out of the chapel door.

Rob looked at Sandy and shrugged. "She spoils those cats."

"It's for the cats?"

Rob laughed. "A whole salmon every day. She buys a frozen one every night on her way home, lets it defrost overnight and then leaves it for the cats while she's at work. Gus orders them specially."

"Wow," Sandy said. "Sounds like they eat better than me."

"And me!" Rob admitted. "I'm on the beans-on-toast-diet most nights. Not that I'm moaning, I can't get enough of it."

"I came to show you these," Sandy said, holding out the watercolour books. "They're new in the shop, I wanted you to have the first offer of them."

Rob took the books from her and flicked through each one. "How much?"

"I was thinking a fiver each, how does that sound?"

"It sounds reasonable, but I don't have a penny change on me. Can I collect them tomorrow? I should be able to squeeze a lunch break in, fingers crossed."

"Well, take the books now and bring the money across whenever," Sandy said, happy to have found a new home for the books at a handsome profit for her and a reasonable price for Rob.

"Very kind. I'll get stuck into these tonight while I have my beans on toast!" Rob said, then glanced around the empty chapel. "I was going to head off shortly but if you wanted any time alone in here, I can stay."

"Oh no, no," Sandy blurted, glancing at the large Jesus again. "I'm all done. Thanks, Rob."

He held the door open for her and she emerged into the cool, dark village as if returning from an otherworldly experience. She remembered the day of her mother's funeral, how she had sat in the front row of the chapel, with Coral on one side of her and their father on the other side. She had focused so much on the patent black shoes she had worn that day, already scuffed despite being just days old, that she could still picture every detail of them to this day. The vicar, a large, hairy man, had spoken for what seemed like hours about some woman, some woman who had done things Sandy had been unaware of. Hearing strangers discuss her mother was something she had to get used to in the years that followed.

Everyone had an opinion about the tragic death.

Easier to focus on the shoes.

Black patent, silver buckle, grey tights peeping through.

The memory made Sandy shudder and the night feel darker, and caused her to turn left out of the church, towards her sister, instead of right, towards home.

7

*R*ight in the middle of the lunch rush, Dorie Slaughter barged into Books and Bakes, dressed in an orange kagool and wearing lipstick of the same shade.

"Good for her!" She said as she joined Jim and Elaine at a table for two.

"Good for who?" Coral asked, from the counter. "And a pot of tea?"

"Oh, go on. I wasn't going to come back in today, but I want to see what happens. She's got guts, that one, but they won't let her get away with it."

"Get away with what?"

"She's reopened the chip shop!" Dorie announced, loud enough for everyone in the cafe to hear, whether they wanted to or not. "Now my son here must have a duty to investigate it, it must be a criminal offence."

Jim blushed. It was his day off and Elaine had persuaded him to have a sit-down lunch with her instead of going to the burger van as he usually did. "I can't comment."

"Of course not, son," Dorie said. "You can tell me later."

Sandy rolled her eyes and opened the cafe's front door.

While she had no interest in village gossip, this could be an important development in her murder investigation. To her horror, as she opened the door, Tom Nelson walked by.

He glanced at her, gave a little wave, but continued walking without saying a single word.

Sandy felt the heat rise through her body and was unsure whether she was more angry or embarrassed. She glanced left and right, to check if anyone had seen her be snubbed, but the street was empty. Taking a deep breath, she strode out of the cafe and turned left towards The Village Fryer.

The lights inside were on and, to her surprise, when she pushed on the door, it opened.

"We're not open yet, give us half an hour." Isabelle Irons called from behind the counter, where she was wearing an apron over a jumper that looked to be cashmere.

"It's ok, I don't want any food. I heard you were open again and thought I'd see if it was true. I'm pleased for you." Sandy said, hoping her smile looked genuine.

"Oh, it's you," Isabelle said. "Still playing cops and robbers?"

"I'm still..."

"I'm not interested. I've got enough on working out how to get this place set up for a shift." Isabelle said.

"Can't you ring one of the staff?" Sandy asked.

"It was hardly planned," Isabelle said. "I haven't had time to ask anyone. I just realised, that horrible man's dead, I can't see how this decision can still stand."

"You mean you haven't got permission to be open again?" Sandy asked, as her nostrils reacted to a smell of rancid oil cooking.

"This is my livelihood, I'm not waiting for the council to hire a replacement and come out and do a proper assessment. Let them give me a telling off. Cripes, can you smell that?"

Sandy nodded. "I think you need to change the oil."

Isabelle sighed. "I should have sold this place, it's brought me nothing but bad luck. I thought, a mobile home park or a chip shop. Why on earth did I choose this?!"

Sandy shrugged.

"Have you got any other suspects yet, then or am I still numero uno?" Isabelle asked, fiddling with switches in an increasingly manic way.

"I... I know he didn't see the attack coming."

"Oh! Move over, DC Sullivan! What an explosive discovery in the case!" Isabelle said.

"Okay then," Sandy said. "If you were me, where would you be focusing."

Isabelle sighed. "I wouldn't be you, for a start, trying to do police work for them, but if I had to play this game, I'd be speaking to the witnesses, of course."

"There aren't any witnesses. I discovered his body, there was nobody else around."

"Oh, Sandy. There are always witnesses. Whether they come forward is another thing altogether. He was killed right on the village square, there must be twenty houses overlooking the scene. People might not talk to the police. But they'd talk to you."

Sandy grinned to herself in disbelief. She couldn't believe she had missed such a vital step. If she was going to solve the case, she had to stop following her hunches as they appeared and investigate - like the police, but with the advantages of her being a local.

"You're right, Isabelle. You're right." She said, and left the woman to her attempts to learn how to run her own business.

**

She hadn't been back in Books and Bakes for over five minutes when the door burst open and Isabelle Irons walked in.

"Is Bernice here?" She asked, her forehead glistening with beads of sweat.

"Bernice!" Coral called. Bernice appeared from the kitchen, took one look at Isabelle and her mouth contorted into a frown.

"What's wrong?" She asked. She clearly didn't have the friendly relationship with Isabelle that she did with Sandy.

"I'm attempting to open the Fryer." She began. "And I may need a little help. Are you free?"

Bernice glanced down at the apron she was wearing, then back up at Isabelle. "No, I'm at work."

"I'm sure Sandy could manage without you for five minutes..." Isabelle said.

Sandy bit her lip. She didn't like being placed in situations like this, where her co-operation was assumed, but she didn't want to be difficult and cause Bernice problems. "We'll be ok for five minutes, but that's all. We're really busy today."

"Five minutes will be perfectly sufficient, I'll have everything under control easily then," Isabelle said, then returned her gaze to Bernice. "Come on, chop chop!"

She left Books and Bakes and Bernice followed, casting Sandy a look that was gratitude or frustration.

"She runs that place like a dictatorship." Benedict

Harlow said, to Sandy's surprise. He and his wife Penelope were eating jacket potatoes with their son Sebastian.

"Benedict." Penelope scolded. As Waterfell Tweed's closest thing to the aristocracy, the Harlow family distanced themselves from gossip and turmoil. Or at least they had until their lives were affected by two murders.

"He's not wrong." Dorie Slaughter called. "Fancy coming and pulling poor Bernice from one workplace to sort another. She should know how to get her own business set up for the day?"

"Some business owners aren't that hands on." Sandy said, with a shrug. She agreed that it was strange but didn't want to throw flames on the subject. There wasn't a single element of her business that she didn't understand how to do. Bernice was a more talented baker, and Coral was a natural saleswoman, but Sandy was capable of preparing the food and running the till, and everything else too.

"I wonder why DC Sullivan hasn't charged her yet," Dorie muttered in between bites of a sausage sandwich.

"Think she did it?" Coral asked.

"Course she did!" Dorie said. "Closed her chip shop down, didn't he? She gets him out of the way and then opens her shop again. It's obvious. If they'd just let my Jim lead the case, it'd all be solved by now."

"Do you think she did it, Jim?" Coral asked.

Jim's cheeks flushed, which was common whenever he was asked a direct question. "I don't know, and I can't talk about it."

"He has to be discrete, my Jim does," Dorie said, as she reached across the table and patted his arm. Jim winced and Elaine stiffened and moved closer to him. "Of course, he can tell me things as his mother, things I could never repeat in here."

"Dorie, Jim can't tell either of us about police business. You shouldn't say things like that or you'll get him in trouble." Elaine said. Her timid voice was rarely heard in a confrontation and the whole of her chest and neck flushed a deep pink as she spoke.

"He might not trust you enough to divulge important information, missy, but I've been around a lot longer than you have," Dorie said. "You shouldn't let your fancy woman speak to me that way, James."

Jim sank as low as he could in his seat, clearly wishing the ground would open and swallow him whole. Elaine, to her credit, said nothing more, but Sandy couldn't help but imagine the trouble he would be in with both women back at home.

"Anyway..." Coral said. "About the murder. If Isabelle had done it, do you think she'd draw attention to herself by opening the chip shop again?"

It was a good point, Sandy thought.

Dorie shrugged. Her interest in Isabelle's guilt had been overtaken by a need to sulk.

Coral turned to Sandy and raised her eyebrows.

"I'm going to head out later, I want to speak to some more people about the murder," Sandy whispered to her sister. Coral's eyes opened wide.

"Suspects?" She mouthed.

"Witnesses." Sandy corrected.

"Please be careful," Coral said, reaching across and giving her hand a squeeze. "Sorry, I didn't mean to be all Dorie on you, I just worry about you."

Sandy's laugh was interrupted as the door burst open, the bell ringing to signal the person's arrival. Sandy looked across to see Bernice, her cheeks rosy red and her mouth set firm in a stern line.

"All sorted?" Sandy asked with a sympathetic smile. She had worked for some awful bosses herself and had always tried to be more understanding with her staff.

"I've rung one of the young girls to come in and sort it," Bernice explained, then walked straight past the counter and back into the kitchen. The dirty dishes were neverending. Sandy knew she would have to consider investing in a commercial dishwasher, but she had no idea where she would fit one in the tiny kitchen and she didn't have the budget (or the landlord's permission!) to extend the premises.

"I'm going to get off then, you'll be ok?" Sandy asked.

Coral had just taken an order from a customer Sandy hadn't seen before, and her attention was focused on the coffee machine that she was still nervous about using. The look of panic in her eyes made Sandy stifle a giggle. Coral was so confident when it came to convincing customers to add extra items to their orders, but the coffee machine stumped her every day.

"Need some help?" She asked.

"I'll get my head around it one day, I'm sure!" Coral said with false bravado. Sandy knew she was desperate to prove herself as a valuable employee and was conscious of any mistakes she made. On one of her first days, she had given a customer £20 change when he had paid with a £20 note and when the mistake had been discovered as they cashed up she had burst into tears.

"Come on, what is it?"

"It's a hazelnut latte. If it was a cappuccino, I'd be fine I think." Coral said. She stepped to one side to allow Sandy to take over and demonstrate how the drink was made.

"There's so much choice, that's the problem," Sandy said. "I took months to remember the names of them all;

mochas and macchiatos, cappuccinos and cortados, and then the syrups and the extra shots and the almond milk crowd. You'll get your head around it all, don't worry."

Coral flashed her a grateful smile and took the cup from Sandy's hand to deliver to the customer.

"I can stay?" Sandy asked when Coral returned behind the counter.

"No, it's fine, honest... I know what it's like to be on the tail of a story." Coral said, referring to her past as a journalist. "You catch the bad guys, and I'll stay here and study the coffee machine manual a bit more!"

8

*W*rapped up in her yellow mac and chunky scarf, Sandy braved the outside. She walked into the middle of the village green and looked around, her eyes taking in each building that offered a view of the place where Dick Jacobs was murdered.

The village green was surrounded on four sides by a mix of cottages and businesses. Books and Bakes sat on High Street and looked out over the green, as did other shops and businesses including The Tweed. The Village Fryer was a few doors to the left of Books and Bakes with a view of the green obstructed by the doctor's surgery, which took up the whole length of the village green along which she had found Dick Jacobs.

The length opposite the surgery was taken up with the library, which kept odd opening hours and was never open later than 4 pm, and a cottage that had no windows overlooking the green.

Opposite High Street was Manor Way, the road which lead to Waterfell Manor. Gus' butchers and Cass' LA Nails were on Manor Way, and so were several cottages. Rob

Fields, Cherry Gentry, and Dorie Slaughter lived on that road, as did Coral.

Sandy decided the best plan was to take a lap of the green and speak to as many people as she could.

It was 2.30pm and to her surprise, the newsagent next to Books and Bakes was closed. A tatty piece of paper with 'GONE FOR LUNCH, BACK IN AN HOUR' scrawled on it was stuck in the window. The next shop was a charity shop that had even more restricted opening hours than the library. The opening times sign in the window suggested the shop should have been open at 2.30pm on a Thursday, but in reality, Sandy couldn't remember seeing it open for weeks and suspected the woman who owned it chose her operating hours day by day as the mood took her.

Sandy stood outside the next building and took a deep breath. Her throat tightened as sadness tore at her chest. Just a few days earlier, thinking of Tom Nelson or the prospect of seeing him made a warmth spread through her, and now she winced at the knowledge that she had to speak to him.

Gulping down her nerves, she pushed open the heavy door and walked into the heat of the pub. A fire crackled away and the ring of laughter was in the air. A table of men who Sandy recognised by face only were supping a pint of dark ale each and pointing to some sporting match being shown on the large TV.

Sandy walked past them unnoticed and stood at the empty bar for a few moments until Tom emerged from the back with a cardboard box in his arms. Sandy watched him for the few seconds before he noticed her, how at ease he was with his work, how easily he tore open the tape that sealed the box and took out various crisps and nuts to restock the snack tubs behind the bar.

Eventually, she coughed to alert him to her presence, and the spell was broken. He stiffened and gave a terse smile.

"Sandy." He said as he returned the crisps to the box and walked down the bar towards her. "What can I get for you?"

"Oh, nothing, thanks, Tom." She said, his name feeling foreign on her lips. "I wanted to have a chat with you, do you have a few minutes?"

Tom glanced around the pub. Apart from the table of men, the place was empty.

He nodded to her. "Let's grab a booth."

Sandy allowed him to lead her to a booth in the corner of the pub and let Tom sit at an angle that allowed him to watch the door to see if anyone came in.

"So... you're ok?" She asked. Making small talk had never been a strength of hers. She'd much rather speak about things that mattered than discuss the weather.

Tom nodded, not taking his eyes off the door. "You?"

Sandy sighed. "I'm fine. Look, I'm here about Dick Jacobs."

The colour blanched from Tom's face at the mention of the dead man. "What's that got to do with me?"

"Nothing." Sandy scoffed. "I found him, Tom. I found his body. And I'm going to find his killer."

Tom groaned and met her gaze. "I didn't know you'd found him. I'm sorry."

Sandy shrugged. Even his sympathy seemed forced, stiff. "I'm speaking to everyone who might have seen something. Your windows look out over the surgery. Someone in here could have seen something. Will you help me?"

To her surprise, Tom shook his head. "I can't. I don't know anything. It's not like I sit looking out of the window when I'm in here, I'm at the bar or in the back. Monday night I was sorting the deliveries, I wasn't even in here. Speak to Tanya if you want, but we don't know anything."

Sandy nodded, noting the ease with which he described him and the barmaid as a 'we'. She stood up as disappointment sagged through her. "Ok. I get it. I get it."

"Sandy!" Tom called after her, but she walked out of the pub without looking back.

By the time she reached the next house on her list, her cheeks were damp with tears. She continued walking until she reached LA Nails, where she looked in the window and saw Cass sat sorting through paperwork. She pushed open the door as a sob choked its way out of her throat, causing Cass to gaze up from her work and rush over to engulf her in a hug.

"Oh my darling, what's happened to you?" Cass asked as Sandy allowed herself to release all of the tears she had been storing. Finally, they slowed, and Cass lead her to the settee that was meant for customers to wait on, and disappeared into the back to make them a drink.

"I'm so sorry to turn up like this while you're working," Sandy said when she returned with a mug of mocha for her and a black coffee for herself. She smiled at the thought that her best friend had gone to the trouble of having her favourite drink in for her occasional visits.

"Oh, shush. What's happened, Sand?"

"I feel so silly, it's nothing, I've just overthought everything and got my feelings heart."

"So it's a man. Is it Tom Nelson?" Cass asked. Sandy laughed at how quick she had worked it out, then the laugh transformed into tears. "Well, I don't know what he's done, but he's been acting strangely."

"Strange?" Sandy asked. Cass didn't have much to do

with Tom so she couldn't imagine how Cass could have noticed his behaviour change.

"I saw him on the square Monday night when I was locking up, he was just pacing up and down. In a world of his own, he was. I called out to him, I didn't realise he'd upset you then or I'd have done more than say hello to him! He didn't even acknowledge me."

A shudder ran through Sandy's body. "Monday night? What time?"

"Ooh I don't know Sand, you know what I'm like with time. I was ran off my feet in here all day so it must have been half five? Six?"

Sandy pulled her notebook from her bag and scribbled down what Cass had just told her, her heart racing in her chest.

"What did I say?" Cass asked.

"Nothing," Sandy said, reluctant to share her suspicions until she knew more. "Cass, I need to go."

"No way lady - oh listen to me - I'm talking like Derrick now!" Cass said with a laugh. "You're staying here until you tell me what's wrong."

Sandy sighed. "I can't even explain it without feeling like I'm a teenager again, Cass. But I thought things were going well with Tom, and then he just changed. He hasn't spoken to me for days. No messages, no suggestion that we see each other again, nothing. And I've just been into The Tweed to see him and it was so strange. I just don't understand what changed or what I've done wrong."

"Hey!" Cass said. She moved from the settee to sit on the floor in front of Sandy, her legs crossed underneath her. "You've done nothing wrong, I can tell you that. You're the loveliest, kindest woman there is. If Tom doesn't want to see you again, firstly he should have the guts to tell you that and second, it's his loss."

"You say that Cass but why have I been single for so long if I'm so lovely and kind?"

"Erm... that's easy, Sand. There's hardly a huge supply of eligible bachelors around in Waterfell Tweed, and you've been so focused on Books and Bakes you've not put yourself out there. You only got friendly with Tom while you were trying to solve a murder!"

Sandy looked down at Cass. "I've never thought of it like that. Do you think he got tired of me not making enough time for him?"

Cass shrugged. "I don't know. Was he asking to see you more?"

"Not really," Sandy admitted. "It wasn't serious, I mean we weren't even dating. We just saw each other on our days off sometimes."

"Had you even kissed him?" Cass asked.

Sandy's cheeks flushed. "Not really. I thought he was taking it slow... oh no!"

"What?"

"What if I misread the whole thing and he was just being a friend? I bet he's backed off because I was misreading the signals so badly. I'm such a moron."

"You're not a moron," Cass said. "But, maybe this is a sign that you want a relationship after all. You've spent so long being miss independent, all happy on your own and stuff, but maybe you'd like a man. I mean, I know I would."

"You would?" Sandy asked. She had thought that both she and Cass were determined they didn't need men.

Cass shrugged. "I'm not going to start online dating or anything like Coral, but yeah, if the right man appears, I'd like it. I'd like the company. I mean, it's coming to something when my 15-year-old sister's got a better love life than me. Derrick bought her flowers the other night!"

"Hold on, Coral told you she's online dating?" Sandy asked. Bernice had made her aware but she was disappointed that her sister would tell Cass but not her.

Cass snorted a laugh. "I caught her. Needed to use her phone when she came in for her last appointment, mine hadn't got signal, so she handed it to me and the page opens on to a dating app. She was mortified so don't tell her you know."

"I guess we're all a bit more lonely than we've been admitting," Sandy said.

"Not lonely, Sand. I'm not lonely. Truth is, with this place and Olivia and seeing my friends, I don't know how I'd fit a man in. I guess you just make space, though, don't you."

"I'm sure you wouldn't have thought you'd got the room in your life for a teenage sister a while ago," Sandy said. "I keep thinking how amazing you're doing with Olivia, and I've never told you. I should tell you more. You're doing a good job."

Cass grinned. "Aww, thanks. She's a good kid. Can't imagine life without her now."

Sandy cried again. "That's how I feel about Tom. Isn't that pathetic?"

"It is a little bit, yeah," Cass said, and her bluntness made them both laugh. It was one thing Sandy loved most about her best friend, that she was always honest with her, even if a white lie might be more sensitive and less painful. She always knew she was getting the truth from Cass, and isn't that what a best friend is for?

She scooped Cass up in a hug, feeling the familiar shape of her bones and curves.

"I love you." She whispered.

9
———

*T*he alarm woke Sandy from a deep sleep and a dream that her hair had turned grey overnight. In the dream, she had been plucking every grey strand of hair out of her head with tweezers, until she was bald.

Sandy jumped from the bed and raced into the small bathroom, where she gazed at her reflection in the mirror. Her hair was still dark brown, but there were two new grey hairs sitting on the top of her scalp. She had plucked three out before bed the night before, no doubt where the dream had come from, but realised that if she continued plucking, she would slowly grow bald.

With a sigh, she padded downstairs and got her diary out of her handbag, then wrote herself a note to make a hair appointment. She felt too young to need to dye her hair, and the realisation that she was going grey was poorly timed with the certainty she now felt that she had scared Tom Nelson off by not realising he was only interested in friendship.

She showered, dressed in deep blue jeans and her favourite 'I Love Waterfell Tweed' t-shirt and left the cottage. As soon as she was in her driveway, she could hear the commotion from next door, and tried to pretend she couldn't.

"Dorie, please, just leave it for me to sort," Elaine called from inside the cottage, where the front door was wide open.

"We can't live like this Elaine. Did your mother not teach you how to keep a home?" Dorie responded from outside.

"I was going to take it to the bin on my way out with Scamp!" Elaine called as she appeared on the front doorstep.

"For Heaven's sake, Elaine, rubbish can't stay outside the door for the entire world to see. Imagine what the neighbours will say."

"I was fetching the lead!"

Sandy smiled to herself, shook her head and got in her car. Elaine was a brave woman agreeing to allow Dorie to move in with her and Jim. She turned on the ignition, which made both Elaine and Dorie turn their attention to her. Sandy kept her gaze away from them, not wanting them to realise she had heard them, and drove away.

The short drive to Books and Bakes gave her time to calm her mind from the crazy dream and consider her next actions. Sandy still had potential witnesses to speak to, and she needed to put aside her feelings and consider whether Tom could be involved in the murder. She felt out of her depth and overwhelmed and decided she needed to make progress, and fast.

After she parked her car, Sandy poked her head in the door at Books and Bakes. It wasn't opening time yet, and she could smell the day's baking and see Coral wiping down tables.

"Hey." She called. Coral turned to look at her and gave

her a smile. When had her sister began online dating in secret, Sandy wondered, but put the thought out of her mind. "I'm going to carry on speaking to people, I'll be in before the lunch rush."

"Ok Detective," Coral said with a smile. "Stay safe."

Sandy rolled her eyes but flashed her sister a grin. It was nice to be cared about.

She turned left out of the shop, past the disused Community Centre next door and the off-license next to that. The off-license opened in the afternoon, she would have to go in there another time. The Village Fryer had been closed on the night of Dick Jacobs' murder, so she had crossed the building off her list.

She crossed the road and forced herself to walk up to the spot where she had found the man's body. When she had reached what she thought was the exact spot, she forced herself to slowly turn 360 degrees. Whoever had killed him must have seen him standing or walking there and seen their opportunity, then crept up and struck him to the head.

What had been the murder weapon, Sandy asked herself, but she had no idea where to start with ideas. Surely, anything hard could knock an unsuspecting man to the ground if enough force was used. The blow didn't even have to kill him, the fall to the floor could have done that. She wished that DC Sullivan was more open to discussing the case with her, but she knew he wouldn't reveal a single thing to her, and she didn't think it would be fair to ask Jim Slaughter to tell her anything. She also suspected he knew little about the case.

Taking a deep breath, she continued walking and pushed open the door to the doctor's surgery. The receptionist was a bulldog of a woman named Gertrude Taylor. She saw it as her one and only job to protect the doctor from as many people as possible, protecting her time as if treating ill people was a huge time-drain for the GP and not her profession.

She ruled the surgery alone, boasting about her refusal to allow another receptionist to assist with the workload and going years without a holiday. Her strategy, as disliked as it was by the ill people who needed to see Dr. Lydia Emmanuel, appeared to be successful as the surgery had expanded over the years, introducing various locum doctors and other medics to the practice and offering a wide range of minor surgeries and physical therapies on site. It had grown into a far better doctor's surgery than a village the size of Waterfell Tweed could expect, and Gertrude Taylor was not scared of telling people how instrumental her role had been in creating it.

"Morning, Gertrude," Sandy said, feeling the chill inside the room. The walls were covered with noticeboards with Gertrude used to passive-aggressively communicate various messages. "NO, WE WON'T TURN THE HEAT UP: HEAT SPREADS GERMS" one sign declared.

"You don't have an appointment," Gertrude said, without the need to check the appointment lists.

"No, I don't, I just wanted to remind myself what time you're open until on Mondays?" Sandy asked.

"Opening times are on the board," Gertrude said, gesturing across to the third noticeboard in a row of at least seven.

Sandy read that they closed at 5 pm on Mondays, as she had expected. "A place this modern must have CCTV, am I right?"

"Of course. And we do prosecute if anyone's abusive." Gertrude said. That was true, Sandy knew. Dorie Slaughter had been interviewed by her own son a few years ago after storming out of the surgery in a rage when her prescription wasn't ready at the normal time. It had gone no further than a police interview, but Dorie had never forgiven Gertrude.

"How about the outside? CCTV out there too?"

The question stopped Gertrude in her tracks. She usually had an answer for everything. "Why do you ask?"

"I was just passing and thinking about all that graffiti that happened to the butcher's." Sandy lied. "And I thought this is such a nice building, I bet it could be a target. But I know you've got everything covered, Gertrude. I needn't have worried."

"Actually," Gertrude said, casting a glance behind her to check they weren't being overheard. "You're right, it's in hand. I think they're coming next week to install it."

"Oh, excellent. See, I knew you'd have it sorted. I'll leave you to it." Sandy said. She left the building and took out her notebook, turning to the page where she had written a list of every building she wanted to visit. She crossed the surgery off the list. Gertrude's hesitation about the date of the installation told Sandy there was no outside CCTV and no plan to install any, although she suspected Gertrude would change that now she had the idea in her mind.

She continued walking and opened the rickety gate that led down the path to Rob Fields' cottage, where she gave two soft knocks on the door. She had never visited the vicar at his home before and had no idea about his comings and goings. After a few moments, she heard movement inside and smiled as he opened the door.

It was strange to see him without his dog collar on, and even more strange to see him wrapped in a fleeced blue dressing gown and slippers. It was still before 9 am, and Sandy felt guilty for disturbing him so early in the day.

"Sandy, what a surprise," Rob said, gesturing to his clothes with a shrug and a wide smile. "Come on in."

He lead her through to the sitting room, the very room which Sandy had expected to overlook the pavement outside the surgery. As she walked in, she realised that the view from the window was of the side of the doctor's surgery, and some of the village green. The pavement along the other side of the surgery wasn't visible at all.

"I hate to say this, Rob, but I think I've wasted your time," Sandy said, turning to him with an apologetic smile.

"Well, perhaps not your place to say. I believe there's always a greater plan. Why don't you tell me what you were here for and we'll see together if it's been a waste or not?"

Sandy nodded and took a seat. To her surprise, Rob's cottage was modern and as a bachelor pad should be. Leather reclining chairs in a faded mahogany shade were spread around a coffee table covered in papers, a bowl of half-eaten cereal and spare change, and faced towards a small TV.

"I'm investigating Dick Jacobs' murder," Sandy said. She paused to allow the vicar to protest and tell her to leave it to the police, but he didn't. "I thought your cottage would have a view of the pavement outside the doctor's but it hasn't."

"You wondered if I'd seen anything?" Rob asked.

"Exactly."

"Well, as you say, my view's obscured well by the monstrosity of the surgery itself," Rob said with a smile. "And on Monday evening, I was in the chapel not at home. I'd been, let's say, distracted from my work in the day and needed to get caught up."

Sandy nodded. "Did you know him at all?"

"Never spoke to him," Rob said. "I heard plenty about

him, Cherry had some run-ins with him, and I know Gus did too."

"He wanted to close the butcher's," Sandy said. "I didn't know he had an issue with Cherry? Was he suggesting there was a problem with the church?"

"Oh no!" Rob exclaimed. "Maybe he was a God-fearing man, the church was never on his radar. He objected to Cherry's cats."

"Cats?" Sandy asked. "Was he a dog person?"

"He apparently had received complaints about the noise and the mess caused by Cherry's cats, which was a little hard to believe as they're indoor animals and really very clean. Then it escalated into him having complaints about the welfare of the animals. He said he couldn't really deal with that, it was more of an RSPCA matter."

"He wanted to upset as many people as possible, it seems," Sandy said.

"I can't agree with you there, Sandy. He was doing his best, just like all of us are. I heard rumours that his job had been so target driven that he had to close down more and more businesses year on year or he'd lose his job. I believe that's why he was off ill for so long."

"I thought he had a secondment to another department?" Sandy asked.

Rob shrugged. "We've heard different things, then, and who knows the truth."

"Well, I should let you get back to your breakfast," Sandy said, gesturing to the cereal bowl on the table.

Rob let out an awkward laugh. "That was last night's supper actually!"

10

*S*andy left the vicar's house and walked into a torrent of unpredicted rain. Grateful for her trusty yellow mac, she pulled the hood up and ran into the butcher's next door.

Gus looked up at her from his work slicing a huge joint of meat and burst into a laugh. "Nice weather for it! You look like a jolly fisherman bursting in here like that. What's up, missed your ship?"

Sandy was used to the fisherman comments aimed at her coat. She didn't care about them at all, she was proud of her bright jacket that very often gave the only splash of colour to her black outfits.

"Haha, everyone's a comedian aren't they." She said with a good-natured smile. Gus had had his personal demons to fight, seeing him so happy was a nice change. "I wondered if I could have a chat, about Dick Jacobs?"

"Urgh." Gus groaned, his good mood seeming to disappear in an instant. "I thought I'd heard the last of that name. You investigating?"

"I'm trying to speak to everyone who might have seen something that night."

"Can't help ya," Gus said, as his attention returned to slicing meat. "I was still here but I was in the back cleaning everything up."

"You were here? I thought you'd have been closed by that time." Sandy said. She didn't use the butcher's much. The regular meat order she had was delivered to the shop each week before it opened, and she rarely went to the trouble of cooking meat just for herself at home.

"You know what it's like, Sand. If a customer comes in, you don't turn them away. I think I left here at seven, saw the police tape and stuff but thought it wasn't my business. I never thought it was another bloomin' murder." Gus explained. He shook his head as he spoke and gazed out of the window towards the spot outside the surgery where Dick Jacobs had been killed. His shop window offered a direct, unobstructed view of the scene. He was the person most able to have witnessed something and had seen nothing.

"Did you not see anything at all that was unusual, Gus? Anything?"

The man shrugged. "It was a normal Monday, rushed off my feet all day. I didn't have time to notice if anything was unusual, to be honest."

"Okay. Well, if you think of anything, let me know."

"They've already been and done this, ya know? The police." Gus said as Sandy turned to walk away.

"What did you tell them?" She asked.

"Same as I've told you." He said, giving her one last shrug as she walked out of the shop.

Prepared for the rain this time, she pulled up her hood before opening the door, and sprinted across to the cottage next door, where Cherry Gentry lived. She banged on the door a lot harder than she had on Rob Fields' when it was dry, and Cherry raced to the door, perhaps expecting some kind of religious emergency.

"What?" She asked as she opened the door and saw Sandy, like a bedraggled fisherman, on her doorstep.

"Can I come in?" Sandy asked. She tried to sound pleasant but the rain was hammering on her coat with such fury she wondered if it would continue to keep her dry.

Cherry held the door open and Sandy stepped into the stifling warmth of the cottage. Three cats sat on the staircase watching her. The black one yawned at her and the other two, both tabbies, dismissed her and pawed down the cottage into the back room.

"Well, follow them then," Cherry commanded. Sandy did as she was told. She had never been in Cherry's house before and tried to take in the decor. It was old-fashioned, floral wallpaper and high-back chairs, net curtains up at the windows and a chest freezer stood in the corner of the back room, next to a dining table with two chairs. "If you're here to talk about how Dorie spoke to me, it's really not your place. She can apologise herself."

"Oh," Sandy said, as she realised that Cherry was talking about the incident that had occurred earlier in the week in Books and Bakes. Sandy had forgotten all about it. "No, no, I won't get involved in that. This is a lovely room, Cherry. Do you spend much time in here?"

Cherry appeared puzzled by the question. "Well, I live here."

"Good point! I just meant, lots of people use their front living rooms, but this is such a lovely space, very homely." Sandy said, flailing for the right words. She would have to be less direct in her approach to Cherry, who she didn't know well.

"Never go in the front. I grew up with front room being for best, and I have little use for best." Cherry explained. Sandy's heart sank. Another person with a good view of the murder, who had spent the whole night sitting in the wrong room of the house to see anything other than an inch of the small garden below the net curtain hanging in the back room window.

"Well, this is really nice. I was just speaking to Rob and he mentioned you'd had some problems with Dick Jacobs."

"Not true," Cherry said. She neither sat down nor invited Sandy to, so they both remained standing in the small room. Sandy noticed that the chairs in the room were taken up by cats of all colours and breeds. A regal-looking Siamese sat up and watched her from the dining table. Sandy had to agree with Rob, they all looked very clean and well-groomed.

"Oh?"

"I had no problem with him. He had a problem with my babies." Cherry said. She bent and scooped up a grey cat with one eye. "Silly man, hey Sugar, not liking the babies."

"What happened to his eye?" Sandy asked.

"Fox got her. They don't go out now, the world's too dangerous for them. They stay here with mummy, don't you? Yes, you do. Stay here with mummy." Cherry cooed as she stroked the cat, who purred in appreciation at the attention. Sandy smiled to herself. She wondered if she would end up being a crazy cat lady herself if she remained single.

"They look very happy," Sandy said. "I was going to ask if you saw anything unusual the night Dick Jacobs was killed, but I guess from in here you wouldn't have seen anything?"

Cherry glanced at the floor and Sandy followed her gaze. Three more cats were eating pink salmon from a large bowl, smacking their lips if such a thing was even possible. "Such noisy eaters. Means you're enjoying it, babies doesn't it."

Sandy waited, watching the scene with as much interest as she could gather.

Cherry turned her attention back to Sandy after a few moments of watching her beloved babies eat. "Monday night I watch my soaps. Get home early to sort the babies, they miss mummy all day, give them a love and watch TV in here. Never go in the front, want to see it?"

The offer surprised Sandy, but she accepted. She knew that keeping one room for special occasions, or grown-ups only, had been a popular idea decades earlier. It was a sad thought to consider that Cherry had decided that half of her home's living space was only to be used on special occasions she never had.

She followed Cherry back down the hallway and into the front room, which Cherry unlocked with a key before opening. The room was incredible. A formal dining table with six seats was squeezed into the small room somehow, with place settings for six people, complete with three knives and forks for each person. A chandelier hung above the table, and the window was draped with thick gold curtains and an elaborate lace net curtain.

"Wow, Cherry, this is amazing," Sandy admitted.

Cherry burst with pride. "For dinner parties. My mother always told me a lady is prepared at all times for a dinner party."

"And you're certainly prepared. The dinner parties in here must be wonderful." Sandy said.

Cherry's expression clouded for a moment, then she shook her head and gave Sandy a smile. "They will be."

**

With Dorie's cottage empty, a For Rent sign standing on the small lawn, and Coral at work at Books and Bakes, there was nowhere else for Sandy to go apart from The Tweed again, to see if Tanya was working.

She pushed open the door and almost fell into Tom Nelson's arms.

"Sandy!" He exclaimed, his cheeks flushed with colour. He had taken hold of her by her waist to stop her barging into him, and for a moment his hands remained on her. Her heart skittered until he removed his hands and stepped to the side to allow her to pass.

"Sorry, Tom. Always going a million miles an hour, aren't I?" She said, with a smile.

He focused his gaze down on the floor and gave an awkward cough. "Aren't we all? I'm just off out, Tanya's around."

And with that, he was gone.

Sandy took a deep breath and walked through the bar, where Tanya was drying glasses and hanging them in place above the bar. She greeted Sandy with an easy, uncomplicated smile.

"Early in the day for you Sandy, everything okay?" Tanya asked.

"I don't know," Sandy admitted, plonking herself down on a bar stool. "I just don't know."

"Wanna tell me all about it? I've had plenty drunker than you come in and bare their soul..."

"No, no, I'm fine," Sandy said. She shook her head in an attempt to clear her mind, to throw some of the thoughts out of her head. Tanya eyed her with concern. "I came in to talk about Dick Jacobs, I'm trying to see if anyone saw anything unusual when he was killed."

"What day was it again?" My memory's like a sieve, honest, every day feels the same." Tanya said. She was a bubbly, upbeat woman. Her personality made Sandy think of candyfloss. She was an ideal barmaid.

"It was Monday, around 6 pm."

"I was here," Tanya said. "Can't remember anything unusual, I don't think. Can't remember anything at all actually! I'd be an awful witness, wouldn't I?"

Sandy smiled. She knew what Tanya meant. The days blurred into each other.

"Okay, well thanks anyway," Sandy said, and then, unable to resist, she continued talking. "Where was Tom off to?"

Tanya rolled her eyes. "I don't know what's got into that man of yours. Honest."

Sandy blushed at the description of Tom as her man. Maybe she wasn't the only one who had thought their relationship had been romantic, after all. "What do you mean?"

"Something's rattled him. I've never seen him like it before. I mean, talk about Dick Jacobs, he didn't help things."

"What do you mean?" Sandy asked.

"Coming in here threatening to close us down, saying we're a noise nuisance or something rubbish like that. That was Monday actually, I think. Yeah, yeah, it was. Tom went after him to see what he meant because Dick Jacobs always says - said - he's got complaints but won't tell you who made them, so Tom went to see who made the complaint. Never found him. And we know why, don't we, someone had killed him. Nasty little man but he didn't deserve that."

"You're saying that he threatened to close The Tweed on the day he was killed?" Sandy asked as a chill ran through her body.

"Exactly. And Tom's never been the same since." Tanya said. "Sort him out, eh, Sand. Have a word with him?"

Sandy tried to smile but her head was swimming with thoughts she didn't want to acknowledge. Silently, she stood up and turned from the bar.

"We need to talk," Coral said, standing by the pub door.

11

"*How* ow did you know where I was?" Sandy asked as Coral lead her out of The Tweed and into the street, where the rain had slowed a little.

"I thought I'd go for a walk at lunch and I saw you come in here, thought maybe we could have lunch together," Coral said. She crossed the road in front of the pub and walked past the library.

"Where are we going?" Sandy asked.

"To mine," Coral said. Her footsteps were heavy and aggressive. She was in a foul mood. Sandy enjoyed the chance to have something to focus on instead of Tanya's words.

She followed Coral to her cottage and into the modern kitchen, and took a seat. Coral paced in front of her, biting a fingernail.

"What's wrong, sis?" Sandy asked. Coral didn't lose her cool often, but when she did, she was completely unable to hide it. If Coral was unhappy, the entire world knew about it. She was keen on typing angry rants on her Facebook profile when someone annoyed her. Sandy always pretended she hadn't seen them.

"What's wrong? You're dating a murderer, that's what's wrong!" Coral said. The colour drained from Sandy's face.

"What! No, I'm not. I'm not even dating anyone but if you mean Tom, he didn't do it."

"I heard what Tanya told you. I can't believe you're making excuses for him." Coral said, and Sandy saw that her eyes were filled with tears. She wasn't angry, she was upset. It was more serious than she had thought.

"Coral, I know him. He would never kill someone." Sandy said although a voice inside her questioned whether she knew him at all. She tried to silence that voice. Tom had been nothing but kind and respectful to her. *Weren't most killers charming,* the voice asked. She groaned.

"You barely know him at all. You've been dating a little, he could pretend to be anyone in that time. We've both known him for years and yet hardly know him at all, isn't that strange?"

"Not really," Sandy said. "He's just shy. Keeps himself to himself."

"You have to give this information to the police," Coral said. Her pacing had intensified in speed. Sandy worried that she might make grooves in the expensive flooring.

"The police have already spoken to everyone. If they suspected Tom, they'd have questioned him, or arrested him."

"I'm done with this game of you playing police, Sandy. It's too dangerous. You need to tell the police what you know, or I will." Coral threatened. Sandy shook her head, stood up from the seat and pulled Coral into a hug.

"I'm being safe." She whispered. "I promise I am."

"No," Coral said. She pulled away from the hug and

shook her head. "You're not changing my mind on this. The police need to be left to do this. Just leave it alone, please?"

Sandy gazed at her sister, at the face she knew so well, and saw the fear written over it. "Fine. I'll leave this one to the police."

Her words made Coral burst into tears and crash into Sandy's arms. "Thank you, thank you. I can't lose you too. I can't lose you too."

The reference to their parents brought a lump to Sandy's throat and she allowed herself to cry. They had experienced too much loss in their short lives. She couldn't do anything to risk Coral being left alone.

**

They walked back to Books and Bakes hand in hand, each exhausted in that way that only comes from sharing high emotions. When Coral had stopped crying, they had sat together in the kitchen, laughing self-consciously until the puffy redness around her eyes reduced a little. Sandy felt like a school child who had been playing hooky as she walked across the village green with her sister.

To Sandy's surprise, when she pushed open the door, Bernice was serving customers.

"What are you doing out here?" Sandy asked. Bernice had been a permanent fixture in the kitchen over recent weeks, either baking or washing pots.

"Boy wonder's taken his job back," Bernice said with a grin.

The curtain that separated the kitchen from the counter

opened and Derrick appeared, an enormous smile plastered across his face.

"Are you well enough to be down here?" Sandy asked.

"Good as new!" He said, and took a dramatic spin behind the counter. He seemed to be pain-free, his movements back to being smooth and easy.

"I'm so happy for you!" Sandy exclaimed.

"Me too," Bernice admitted. "Nice to see the front of house again."

"I couldn't have taken a lunch break otherwise, didn't you realise that?" Coral asked.

Sandy laughed. "No... I didn't. Must have had other things on my mind."

Coral gave her hand a squeeze.

"I guess that means I'm needed upstairs?" Sandy asked. If Derrick was back in the kitchen, the till upstairs in the bookshop was unmanned.

"It sure does," Derrick said. "I never want to sit down again."

"Fair enough," Sandy said with a laugh, and walked through the cafe and up the stairs to her beloved books. A few people were browsing through the aisles, and Derrick had made a 'Please Use The Cafe Till' sign and taken the cash drawer out of the till. Sandy removed the sign and found the cash drawer locked away in the storage room and set it up for use.

Being sat at the counter there, surrounded by books she had amassed herself over a period of years, she felt a calm return to her. Coral's words attempted to break through the peace in her mind but she refused to allow them.

Instead, she grabbed a small box of new stock and carried it out to the counter. She would add them all to the stock catalogue with the handheld scanner while manning the till. The box had been brought in by a young, nervous-looking couple a few days before. Unwanted Christmas presents they had added to their shelves year and year for fear of offending the people who had bought them, they explained. A house move further away from relatives had given them the courage to get rid of the 30-odd brand new books.

"What do you like to read?" Sandy had asked them, curious about their real reading preferences that family appeared to be so ignorant of. The couple had looked at each other and blushed, and for an awkward several seconds neither of them answered.

"We don't like to read." The man had explained. The woman nodded furiously beside him.

"Had to buy a bookshelf for these." The woman added. "Put it up in the living room."

"Do you think that might have made your family think you really liked... erm..." Sandy said, peering into the box to see what the books were. "Er... decoupage?"

The woman gasped and covered her mouth. "Well, I never! I never thought of that! Did you, Graham? Did you think that?"

"I never." The man said, his mouth gaping open.

Sandy had offered the couple £20, a ridiculously low price for so many brand new books on a specialist interest, and they had readily accepted. They were clearly desperate to rid themselves and move on into a book-free chapter of their lives. Sandy had never had a single request for a decoupage book, so was doubtful about whether they would sell, but it was hard to predict what would take a person's fancy.

She scanned them and found a half-empty shelf in the crafts section, where she made them fit.

Then, she sold two books about Yorkshire Terrier dogs to a woman who looked like one herself, complete with a top knot in her hair finished with a bow.

And then she sold three books on fiction writing to a man in a top hat, who didn't say a single word to her during the transaction.

And she sold a single book on military tanks to a man with a ruddy complexion who asked if there was any movement on the price. That question was the one that annoyed her most. It suggested that her pricing structure was plucked out of the air and she always refused to reduce a book's price.

To Sandy, books were precious. One of life's greatest joys and treasures. If she priced her books as low as some customers would like, she'd go out of business, and then where would her customers buy books from? So, she stood her ground and insisted that the price wouldn't be reduced. Most people paid the full price when they saw her determination and Sandy had decided that some people just loved to haggle and try and get a bargain.

The ruddy-faced man huffed and puffed a little but presented a crisp £20 note to pay for the modestly priced £2.99 book. Sandy gave him a winning smile and counted out his change.

She returned to the storage room then to get another box of new stock to catalogue, but saw that there were no boxes in the room. There was no new stock.

She took out her notepad and made a note to remind her to find more stock. Some of the shelves were looking a little empty. Customers were buying books quicker than she was adding to the selection. A good problem to have.

Coral's warning about Tom flashed through her mind suddenly, causing her heart to sink. Could her sister be right? Could gentle, sweet Tom Nelson have killed Dick Jacobs? And if he had, what did that mean about Sandy and her ability to judge a person's character, something she had always prided herself on being able to do both fast and with accuracy.

She groaned and pressed her thumbs into her temples, pushing the thought and the awful questions from her mind.

For the afternoon, she would focus on her books, her business, her wonderful team of friends downstairs who allowed her to dash off and investigate murders while they dealt with customers and cakes and chaos. She would think only of the good things in her life.

For the afternoon.

Difficult decisions could wait for another day.

12

*S*andy gave in after a sleepless night and got up and took a quick shower, turning the water to the highest temperature she could stand and forcing herself to stand under the heat until her body was almost numb. She towel-dried her body and gave her hair a quick dry with the hairdryer, then forced it into a bun and dressed in black leggings and a long black t-shirt.

Having pulled on black knee boots and her yellow mac, she left the cottage, emerging into a still-dark world of silence. She climbed into her creaky old Land Rover and turned on the engine, then drove the short distance to Books and Bakes.

Sandy turned the radio off in the car as the thoughts in her head were deafening on their own, and focused on how the headlights threw light on the dark road. The way her investigation had been designed to throw light on the unknown.

Now, she had learned that switching on a light came with a risk that the things hiding in the darkness may be things she didn't want to see. Thoughts she didn't want to think. Possibilities she didn't want to consider.

There was only one thing to do when she was this anxious.

Bake.

She let herself into Books and Bakes, switched on the lights and locked the door behind her.

She knew what she needed to bake.

She walked into the kitchen and collected the ingredients, then pulled from her handbag the two large bananas she had brought out with her from her fruit bowl at home.

In a large saucepan, she mixed sugar, corn flour, salt, and milk. She mixed for longer than was needed, past the point of the ingredients being smooth, enjoying the task to focus on and the memories it resurfaced for her. Then she cooked the mix over a heat until it became thickened and bubbly before she reduced the heat and continued to cook for two minutes.

She had prepared this recipe so many times over the years that she knew how long was enough with no timer to run down those two minutes for her.

In a separate bowl, she cracked two eggs and beat them, then added a little of the hot mixture to them before returning it all to the pan, where she brought the mixture to a slow, gentle boil, which she continued to cook for two more minutes as she stirred it.

She removed the mix from the heat then and stirred in butter and vanilla extract, creating a custard, which she transferred into a bowl, covered with clingfilm and placed in the fridge. Then she pulled out a ready-made pastry case from the cupboard and placed it in the oven to bake at a low temperature.

She had thirty minutes to wait for the mixture to refrigerate, and a lifetime's thoughts to keep her busy.

Not wanting to face any of them, she returned out front, made herself a large mug of mocha, and took a seat in the cafe, where she forced herself to focus on the smell of the vanilla from the kitchen until she was lost in the memories.

Her parents had been hippies at heart, in love with the idea of an alternative, bohemian lifestyle, but forced to live a more mundane life by the two daughters they had to feed and clothe. The wild spirit her parents had was slowly replaced with a conservative attitude towards spending money, saving money, putting money away for rainy days. The answer to 'can we play' was always 'yes' but the answer to 'can we have' was usually 'no'. Money was tight, so they made their fun at home, and great fun it was.

"Why would we want to leave our lovely home, anyway?" Her mum would say, and it was a good question. Their home was snug, filled with cushions and incense and friends who came and went and were always ready for a tickle match with Sandy and Coral.

The dream of travel never left Sandy's parents, but they began to accept it as being only a dream. Sandy's mum somehow reined in her spirit, and Sandy returned from school one heartbreaking day to see that her mum's long, tousled, sun-kissed hair had been cut to her shoulders and tied into a limp plait.

But there had been one summer, a summer when cousins in the Deep South of the United States of America had issued an invitation, a summer when the car hadn't broken down and the boiler hadn't needed replacing and her father had had a slight promotion. A summer when her mother, who answered every question with a resounding 'yes' or 'why the heck not', received an Air Mail letter asking, 'why don't y'all come?'

And so they did.

Sandy remembered the excitement that had filled the house for weeks beforehand. She had been on two day trips to the seaside before then, and the thought of travelling on an airplane to a brand new country had been unbelievable.

She had little memory of the holiday itself, but she remembered one relative, a cousin or a second cousin, called Connie. She had been as wide as she was tall and Sandy had been certain her clothes had been curtains. She had the prettiest smile Sandy had ever seen on anyone, still.

One day she had whisked Sandy away into her kitchen, bigger than Sandy's whole house, and said, "So I hear y'all like to bake?"

And she had taught Sandy her special recipe.

Banana Cream Pie To Die For.

She'd let Sandy find all of the ingredients in her cavernous fridge and walk-in pantry, presented her with a gift of a wooden spoon with her name etched into it, and stood back to allow her to do all of the mixing, only stepping in when heat was involved. "Your mamma would never forgive me now if we burnt y'all to a crisp, would she, doll?"

Sandy's mother had spent the holiday quiet and they had never returned to see those relatives again, but Sandy had never forgotten baking with Connie.

She smiled at the memory as the timer rang that the thirty minutes was up.

She hadn't remembered that holiday for years. It had never been spoken of after they returned home, and no photographs from the trip were ever displayed or shown to anyone. It suddenly struck Sandy how curious it was that one of the biggest adventures of her childhood had disappeared as if it had been a secret.

She'd have to remember to speak to Coral about it.

But now, her cake needed her.

She returned to the kitchen and took the custard from the fridge, peeling away the clingfilm and taking the ready-prepared pastry case from the oven. It was well done, just how she liked it. She often used the ready-prepared pastry cases instead of baking from scratch but always felt naughty when she did.

She spread half of the custard into the pastry case and then sliced her bananas and arranged them over the filling, then spread the rest of the custard over them. She then measured out a cup of whipped cream and spread it across the top of the pie, then dusted a sprinkling of cinnamon on top of the cream.

The cake smelt glorious and she couldn't resist trailing her finger along the inside of the bowl and tasting the custard mix. She was instantly transported in her mind to Connie's kitchen, to the pride with which she had carried a slice of that cake out onto the porch for her mother, to the way her appearance had snapped her mother out of her thoughts and made her scoop Sandy into a tight embrace. It had been a good, good day.

The pie would need 6 hours in the fridge before it was ready to eat, so it wasn't the best thing to bake in a morning, but she had needed to smell the mix of vanilla, banana, and cinnamon. She had needed to remember that feeling of being so trusted, as she had been in Connie's kitchen.

She wondered where Connie was and if she was still alive. Her childhood mind could not put an age on her, but there was every chance she *would* still be alive.

Just because Sandy's parents had died too young, didn't

mean that everyone had, a thought that could still make Sandy tense with bitterness on her lowest days.

She jumped at the sound of a key in the front door, and peeped through the curtain. *Coral.*

"What time is it?" Sandy asked. Her words made Coral jump.

"Nearly 8. What are you doing here, Bernice said there's plenty of cakes left from yesterday?"

"Banana Cream Pie to Die For," Sandy said, with a smile.

Coral gave a nonchalant nod. "Sounds nice."

"Don't you remember it?"

"Should I?"

"I made it in America, with Connie. Do you remember her?"

Coral burst into a laugh. "I remember her dresses! Mum really got the fashion sense out of the two of them, hey?"

"The two of them? What do you mean?"

Coral narrowed her eyes. "Don't you remember who she was?"

"Yeah... A cousin or something?"

"No, you dork. She was mum's sister." Coral said as she hung her coat up on the stand.

Sandy shook her head in disbelief. "Mum had a sister?"

"You really didn't remember that? That's weird."

Sandy shrugged. "I don't remember much about the holiday, apart from baking this pie with Connie. What do you remember?"

"Well, I remember all of it I guess," Coral said with a shrug. "I remember how hot it got, how sticky my legs felt whenever I went outside. I remember mum painting pictures of trees and wearing flowers in her hair. And I remember you in that kitchen, couldn't get you out of the pantry. It was amazing, though."

"Was mum happy there?"

The question stopped Coral in her tracks. "You know mum, it was always hard to say if she was happy or not. I think she'd wanted to see the world for so long and there she was, seeing it, and it was overwhelming for her."

Sandy nodded. "My memories of her there are her being sad, but I can't say why. I didn't see her crying or anything. I just have this feeling, when I picture her there, that she was sad."

"She was never a crier, she'd just sit quietly, but she'd do the same when she was happy. And then she'd see us and grab us for a dance party or chase us around the house and we'd shriek with laughter. She was fine, Sand, she had a good life."

"Not the life she wanted, though."

"Do any of us?" Coral asked. The conversation was moving towards dangerous territory. "I thought I'd be in London, chasing all the top stories for the national press, and here I am ready to persuade as many people as I can to buy a cake as well as a coffee."

Sandy looked up at her sister. "You could still go to London."

"Oh, stop. I'm fine here, we're fine, mum was fine. Life isn't a fairy tale, that's all. What's got into you, anyway?"

Sandy sighed.

"I was up all night, sis. And I know why I can't handle the thought that Tom might have anything to do with the murder."

"Ok... what is it?" Coral asked, taking a seat next to her sister.

"I love him. I love him, Coral. I'm in love with him!" Sandy said as the tears found her.

13

"It's all gone!" Coral exclaimed as she appeared at the top of the stairs.

Sandy looked at her from the bookshop counter, where she had just finished gift wrapping a book of poetry for Felix, the elderly man who had been in a few days before with his watercolour books.

"What is?" She asked as she mouthed an apology to Felix, who stood waiting for her to wrap the item, his weight supported by his walking stick.

"The banana cream pie! People loved it. You'll have to make it more often." Coral said, then dashed back downstairs.

"Banana cream pie, eh? Sounds unusual." Felix said.

"I was taught to make it in America," Sandy said. She realised the sentence sounded grander than the experience had been. "By an aunt. My aunt."

Felix smiled at her from beneath his moustache. "The best way to learn."

"Is it someone's birthday?" Sandy asked as she handed over the wrapped book to him.

"Oh no, nothing like that. I plan on visiting a lady friend and I was taught not to visit anyone empty-handed."

"Oh, what a lovely thing to be taught," Sandy said. "Well, I hope she likes it."

"Me too," Felix said, with a wink. He turned away and began the slow walk across the bookshop towards the staircase, which he descended with some trepidation.

Sandy returned her attention to the stock report she had been in the middle of doing. The sales figures were the highest they had ever been. Seeing the steady line on the graph that the report created made her beam with pride. Her little bookshop was gaining word of mouth. People were travelling from far and wide to browse her collection, buy new books and then treat themselves to a coffee and cake.

Her happiness quickly turned into panic as she remembered that she had to find new stock if she wanted people to continue visiting and spreading the word. She had haphazardly sourced new stock, and that had worked fine when the shop was less popular, but now she would have to make a committed effort to find new stock more regularly.

She opened her email programme and sent a message to an old friend who had owned a bookshop for decades and who had sold his stock to her when he retired. She asked him to keep his ears open for any news of other stock clearances and gave him a brief update on how business was going.

She was just about to hit send when a voice disturbed her.

"Closed. Closed! Always closed!" The voice came, but Sandy couldn't see anyone.

She stood up from the counter and walked the length of the shop, glancing down each aisle. None of the several customers appeared to be needing any help, so she returned to the counter, where Cherry Gentry was waiting for her.

"Hello, Cherry," Sandy said, with some surprise. Cherry was a dedicated reader, but she had never bought a book from the shop before.

"Library's always closed." Cherry moaned. She held out a single mystery novel for Sandy to scan. "Your mystery section is appalling."

"We don't really do much fiction, Cherry, it's more of the specialist titles. I don't know how this one ended up here, to be honest." Sandy said as she glanced at the book's cover. "Do you only read mysteries?"

"Of course I do," Cherry said as if Sandy was stupid for asking the question.

"That's £3.99."

"£3.99? It's second hand!" Cherry protested. The book was old, with yellowed pages and an inscription written on the inside title page.

"It's why we don't sell fiction, we can't compete with the supermarket prices," Sandy said with an apologetic shrug. She wasn't going to lower the price for a woman who bought a whole salmon every day for her cats.

"Damn the library, what good is it if it's never open?" Cherry muttered.

"I think they're open tomorrow," Sandy said.

"And what good is that? What do I do until then?" Cherry asked. She was becoming increasingly exasperated and the more frustrated she grew, the wider her eyes glared in Sandy's vague direction.

Sandy took a deep breath. "It's up to you, Cherry."

"If I was a God-fearing woman, I'd have a word with Him upstairs about the state of this village," Cherry said.

She unzipped her handbag and pulled out a fabric purse covered in cat hairs.

"You're not a God-fearing woman?" Sandy asked in surprise.

"What's she asking us that for?" Cherry muttered. Sandy had long ago learned that half of the things Cherry said were meant for her own ears only but she was beginning to suspect that Cherry herself wasn't aware that she was saying them out loud. "You're nosey, Sandy Shaw, that's your problem. But since you asked, no, I'm not. Don't believe in any of it. Leave me with my babies and my books and we're fine, need nothing else."

"Isn't it strange working in a church if you don't believe in God?" Sandy asked, unable to resist her curiosity. She had always assumed that Cherry must be religious, to work on what she imagined couldn't be a generous wage in a cold church building.

Cherry shrugged. "I'm not exactly leading Sunday School, am I?"

Sandy smiled to herself and accepted the exact change from Cherry, who immediately turned and stormed towards the lift, carrying her prize in her hand.

As soon as the lift doors opened and she walked in, Sandy's phone rang.

It was her old friend, the retired bookseller.

"Sandy?" He asked. He was out of breath and she could only just hear him over what sounded like wind in the background. After a career of sitting inside, he had devoted his retirement to fell walking and she suspected that's what he was doing. "Perfect timing on the eMail! I got talking to a chap over a Ploughman's the other day and he recognised me from the good old days, told me about a friend of his, closed his shop he has, put it all in storage, can't afford the storage so needs to get rid. Last he said, this friend was getting ready to tip the lot of it, just to get rid. We had a fair chat about the state of bookselling over a pint, I tell ya. Tipping books! Would ya believe?! I can't vouch for the quality or anything, and it's a fair trek for you, but worth a look if ya can get up there quick."

"Wow, thanks, Adrian," Sandy said. "Where is it?"

"Isle of Mull!"

"Isle of Mull? Where's that?" Sandy asked. She'd never heard of the place.

"Scotland! Supposed to be a beautiful little place. I'll send ya this guy's number, ya can sort it with him."

Sandy thanked Adrian and ended the call.

There was no way she could fit in a trip to Scotland. And there was no way she couldn't view a whole shop's stock of books when the seller seemed desperate to get rid.

She took a deep breath and smiled to herself. Some of the shelves were only half-full, so much stock had been sold in the last couple of weeks.

This was the life she had wanted, the life she had dreamed of for so long.

It felt like she was so close to the dream.

The happiness turned her thoughts back to Tom.

How had she allowed herself to fall in love with a man so quickly? So easily? And without realising it was happening?

She picked up her phone and clicked on the text message screen, scrolling down until she found her conversation with Tom. She stood and reread the messages, feeling her stomach flip with the same nervous happiness she had felt as she had received each message.

There were no declarations of love or grand gestures in the messages, but there was an understated back and forth, a gentle intimacy that seemed to be felt by both of them.

Tom was a man of few words, in message as in face-to-face conversations, but he had begun the habit of sending her a text each morning. 'Morning x' it said on most days. Her text messages from Coral and Cass were more emotive and expressive, but based on friendship, not romance. Tom's morning messages, as short as they were, told her that he was thinking of her. That she may have been the first thing he thought of when he woke.

They had stopped without warning, those morning messages. And, too nervous, she hadn't asked why. She hadn't taken the lead and sent one for a change. She had sat back and waited for Tom's next contact.

And she continued to wait.

The next contact had never arrived.

The intimacy felt in those messages, a little secret between them, those morning messages, had been lost.

Could it really be possible that Tom had changed because he had killed a man?

Was Sandy in love with a killer?

14

*S*andy had been gazing at the text message with the bookseller's phone number on for twenty minutes or more, wondering whether to call him or be realistic and accept that there was no space in her schedule for a trip to Scotland. The numbers had begun to blur into each other when she became aware of a man standing at the counter in front of her.

"I'm so sorry!" she blurted out before she realised who it was.

"Hey." Tom Nelson said, moving his gaze from her phone to her face. He looked so handsome that it was painful to look at him and think about what she had lost. He wore a salmon pink polo shirt and faded blue jeans. There was a shaving cut along his jawline.

"Tom." She said. "How can I help?"

Her question made him laugh. "I deserve that. Can we talk somewhere a bit quieter?"

Sandy froze. She didn't want to believe that he was the murderer, but she knew that he had as much motive as Isabelle Irons and that he was in the right place at the right time. That would make him the prime suspect in her case if she could be unbiased. And she had to be unbiased.

"I can't leave here, sorry." She said.

Tom nodded. "Ok. I get it. I'll find you later."

The words sounded ominous and Sandy suddenly didn't want him to find her later. "Talk to me here, it's quiet? I mean, people are browsing, they don't really hang around the till unless they're buying."

Tom shrugged. "I'd rather not speak here, but if you really can't slip out for a few minutes... Ok, I wanted to ask if you'd like to be my date on Valentine's Day."

Sandy felt her knees weaken at his words, and felt relief to be seated.

"A date? Like, a date, date?"

"A date date, me and you. What do you think?" He asked.

"I'd like to, I really would, I'm just not sure what's been..."

"I know I've been acting strange, and I can explain, I promise. Not here, I can't stand here and explain, but if we go out, let me take you out and make it up to you? I'll explain then."

"Is it anything I should be worrying about?" Sandy asked with some trepidation.

Tom laughed and his cheeks flushed crimson. "I hope not."

She realised she would get no more out of him in the public space of the bookshop. "Ok. Yes, then, I'd love to."

"Really?" He asked, and she realised he was nervous. Nervous about asking her on an official date. "Brill, that's great, I'll book a table for us. I'll text you."

"Ok," Sandy said, trying to remain a little reserved.

He grinned and dashed out of the bookshop, taking the stairs three at a time on his way down.

**

As soon as he was out of sight, Coral appeared upstairs.

"Well?" She asked.

"He invited me out for Valentine's Day," Sandy admitted, with a shrug.

"And you said no, I hope."

"Coral, I..."

"I can't believe you've said yes! You promised me, Sand. You promised me you'd stay safe and now you're going out with the murderer himself."

An elderly woman with a foxskin draped across her shoulders turned towards the two of them and raised an eyebrow.

"Ha! You're such a joker, Coral!" Sandy exclaimed as she dragged her sister into the storage room and closed the door after them. "Be quiet, for goodness sake!"

"Sorry," Coral said, sheepish. "I just can't believe you're doing this."

"I'm going on a date," Sandy said. "I told you how I feel about him."

"Oh, Sandy. I already knew how you felt about him! You've been moping about like a teenager because he hasn't texted you, it's been obvious you're in love with him. And it's clouding your ability to see things."

"So, are you saying you're adamant he's the killer?" Sandy asked.

"No!" Coral exclaimed. "I've got no idea who the killer is,

but I do know he was out there around that time, and he had a motive. Not to mention how strange he's been acting since it happened. That all adds up and makes him someone you shouldn't be going out with alone right now, don't you see?"

"I'd better solve this case quick then, so we know one way or the other," Sandy said.

Coral shook her head as a customer pressed the service bell on the counter. Sandy opened the door and saw the foxskin woman holding a small pile of books.

"Let's chat later?" Coral called, flashing a false smile, as she returned downstairs.

**

Sandy didn't expect DC Sullivan to see her, and wondered if the smell of a quality cup of coffee was what brought him out of his room into the police station reception area.

"Sandy Shaw, you remembered." He said, accepting the cup from her. Last time she had visited him at the station, he had told her that in future she should bring coffee since the station's machine served such poor quality drinks.

"I did indeed." She said with a hopeful smile.

DC Sullivan took a sip and nodded his approval. "Very nice. How can I help you?"

"I want to have a chat about the Dick Jacobs case," Sandy said. She expected the officer to roll his eyes or make some sarcastic remark about her sticking her nose in again, but instead, he nodded and gestured for her to follow him down the corridor into his office.

She'd never been in the room before and wondered

what it was used for when the city police weren't in Water-fell Tweed. It was a small room, with a curved desk covered by an old computer and mounds of paperwork, with a swivel chair behind the desk and two plastic chairs stacked on top of each other in the corner. DC Sullivan lifted the top chair and placed it on the other side of his desk and gestured for Sandy to take a seat.

"You didn't bring yourself a coffee, I guess you don't want to try one of ours?" He asked.

"I didn't think I'd be made welcome for long enough to need one," Sandy admitted.

"I'm always open to sensible ideas about solving cases, Ms. Shaw." DC Sullivan said, then took a deep breath. "And, let's face it, you've shown that you do know what you're talking about sometimes."

"Really?" Sandy asked. "Wow. Okay, erm, I've been trying to get my head around it all and something just isn't adding up."

"Welcome to my world." DC Sullivan said.

"Can we have an off-the-record chat, and if I'm anywhere near your thoughts, can you say?"

"It's an active investigation, Ms. Shaw, and you're still not a police officer to my knowledge, but we can... talk." DC Sullivan said. He took a long sip of the coffee, gulping it down in one.

"Okay... I have the cause of death as a blow to the head..." Sandy said and then paused to gauge the officer's reaction. He nodded. "And an attack he didn't see coming. I don't think he tried to fight back or protect himself."

"Mm-hmm." The officer agreed.

"I have no idea at all about the murder weapon," Sandy said. This point was crucial. If the police knew more than she did about the weapon, she needed to persuade DC Sullivan to share his information with her.

"No." DC Sullivan agreed.

"You don't know what it was either?" Sandy asked in surprise. It hadn't occurred to her that she may have worked out exactly as much as the police had. "Wow."

"We learn to take an educated guess in these cases. A skull that's been hit with a hammer looks different to a skull that's been hit with a crowbar, for example. So we can quickly look, in most cases, and see it's a hammer, it's a crowbar, it's a whatever. Before the reports come in and tell us what we already know."

"But you couldn't do that here?" Sandy asked.

DC Sullivan shook his head. Sandy waited for him to elaborate, but he said nothing.

"Surely that means it wasn't any of those weapons you're used to seeing?" Sandy asked.

DC Sullivan raised his eyebrows. "It could mean that."

"OK. And in terms of witnesses, I've spoken to lots of people, and nobody saw anything. Early evening on a Monday, right in the village square, and nobody saw anything, isn't that strange?"

"Could be. Might not be. There's a fact we try to remember in the force - nowt's as queer as folk. Might just be me who remembers it. My dad taught me that phrase. He was in the force, and his dad before him. He'd tell me when I was younger, don't turn everything into a clue. That's what people do. They look too hard for the meaning. It might just be, Sandy, that on a Monday evening everyone's too busy with their own lives to see what's right in front of them."

Sandy blushed at his use of her first name, at the way he was speaking to her almost as a peer, instead of an annoying busybody trying to poke her nose into his case.

"Yeah, I guess that's true. I mean, when I'm at home, I draw my curtains and turn my TV on and anything could happen outside, I guess."

DC Sullivan nodded. "Ok then, the million dollar question. Who are your suspects?"

Sandy gulped. She had been dreading this question and knew she had to somehow dodge it. She couldn't hand Tom over on a plate for DC Sullivan. "Isabelle Irons is the obvious one."

DC Sullivan shook his head. "Alibi."

"Really?" Sandy asked. If Isabelle had an alibi, why hadn't she said that when Sandy went to speak to her?

"Oh yes. Checked it and it holds up."

"I'm out of ideas then," Sandy said.

"You and me both." DC Sullivan admitted. He drank the last of the coffee and tossed the paper cup into the bin by the door.

"Well, I guess that's it then. Thank you for speaking to me, I do appreciate it and I know we haven't always seen eye-to-eye." Sandy said. She stood up to leave.

"Thanks for the coffee." DC Sullivan said, and walked her out.

"Anytime," Sandy said, trying to ignore the feeling of dread in her stomach as she realised that she had a suspect in a case with no other suspects.

**

She returned to Books and Bakes, which was empty apart from one straggler of a customer who nursed a long-since empty drink, and told Derrick, Coral, and Bernice to head home.

"Are you sure?" Coral asked, eyeing her warily.

"Yeah, just go. I'll be fine. I won't be long, hopefully." She said, looking at the customer who showed no signs of being ready to leave.

When the others had gone, she walked through the kitchen, to find that Derrick had washed every single cup, plate, and dish. She allowed a smile. She'd expected there to be a backlog for her to get done. It was good to have him back in the kitchen.

The bell rang out; the last customer must have left.

As she emerged from the kitchen, the sight of a man standing before her made her jump for the second time that day.

"DC Sullivan!" She exclaimed. "You made me jump."

"Sorry." He said, with a coy smile. "I've got a taste for that coffee, wondered if I could have a cup for the journey home. If you're still open?"

"Still open," Sandy said. She turned to make the coffee.

"It was an interesting chat we just had." DC Sullivan said, his voice low. "I'll admit, I was curious to hear your thoughts. See if I'd missed anything. It's not easy, you know, having my cases solved by someone not on the force."

"I never thought of it that way," Sandy admitted. "Sorry. I never meant to step on anyone's toes."

"I know. Doesn't stop questions being asked, though. So, I was curious to see what you'd found out. There's just no clues. It's the perfect crime." DC Sullivan joked.

"Who'd know how to commit the perfect...?" Sandy asked, then froze. Her own words stopped her in her tracks.

She knew who the killer was.

15

"*A*re you okay?" DC Sullivan asked. "You've turned white like a sheet."

"I know who did it," Sandy whispered. "Follow my lead."

"Erm... okay." DC Sullivan said.

"There's no such thing as a perfect murder, right? Everyone leaves a clue." Sandy said. She handed the coffee to the police officer and turned to the machine to make herself a mocha. Her chest had tightened with fear and she needed time to compose herself.

"Well, yeah." DC Sullivan said, his voice uncertain. "It's impossible to kill a person without leaving a trace of evidence that you were there. Whether it's DNA, forensics, a witness, an alibi that falls apart... there's always something."

"And Dick Jacobs had a lot of enemies, right?" Sandy asked. The vague shape of a plan was forming in her mind.

"It looks that way." DC Sullivan agreed. "You know in his office he had a framed award. Not a real one, I'm not sure if he'd mocked it up himself or if someone else did as a joke - it's congratulating him on closing down his 250th business."

"You're kidding? Well, I know he wanted to close the

butcher's, I think that was his next target." Sandy lied. "Have you spoken to Gus Sanders?"

"What we are doing here?" DC Sullivan hissed, his voice low.

"Just talk to me. Make it up if you need to." Sandy said then, seeing the doubt on his face, urged him, "Trust me, please?"

"Gus Sanders, yes, he's a possibility." DC Sullivan said. His voice was stiff, his words clipped and unnatural. Sandy could feel the plan falling apart around her.

"I think it's him," Sandy said, her voice bold and loud. "I think it's Gus."

"Really?" DC Sullivan asked, giving her a stage wink.

"It makes sense. His business was about to be closed down, he's always had a temper on him and it must have got out of control. I think that's it, I think it's him."

"I need to arrest him." DC Sullivan said. "Where do you think he'd be now?"

"Don't go now," Sandy said, shaking her head the tiniest fraction at the police officer. "Go in the morning, to his shop. I bet he's got the weapon stashed there. He wouldn't take it home for his wife to see."

"Good thinking." DC Sullivan said, but it was clear he didn't know how to progress the conversation. Sandy needed to buy time. To continue weaving a web.

"Can I tell you something?" She asked the officer. He nodded. "I saw a crime being committed when I was a child. It was a robbery. We'd gone to the city shopping, me and my sister with our mum, and I was loitering around sulking when I heard this shout, and I turned around and there was a man running through the streets with this bag, like a big black sports bag. And people were chasing him and telling people to call the police, it was back before mobile phones so nobody could really do anything, but I saw the man really clear. He ran right past me and he didn't pay any attention, I was just a kid, I think he even smiled at me. And then I saw in the newspaper a week or so later that the woman who had committed the robbery had been caught. And her photo was there in the paper. I'll never forget her face. Shocks of curly red hair, loads of freckles, bad teeth. And I've thought ever since, how could I have got it so wrong? I saw a man, a man with a big smile, loads of teeth, and it turns out it was a woman. Isn't that mad?" Sandy asked, returning in her mind to the day in question when the man had run past her.

"People make the worst witnesses." DC Sullivan quipped. "Much rather have a nice piece of CCTV or DNA any day. What did she get?"

"Hmm?"

"What sentence did she get?"

"Some kind of community work, the newspaper made a big deal about it being too soft a sentence."

DC Sullivan nodded and smiled. "The plan worked then."

"What do you mean?"

"Just a hunch... but I bet you were right, I bet it was a man. Her boyfriend, her pimp, her dad even maybe. Someone with a longer record than hers, someone who'd have gone straight to prison if they were caught."

"So she just took the blame?" Sandy asked. "Who'd do that? Who'd ask someone to do that?"

DC Sullivan shrugged. "There's another world out there, Sandy, nothing like Waterfell Tweed. There's a world where, if your boyfriend tells you you're handing yourself in, you don't ask any questions."

"Is that the world you're normally working in?" She asked.

He grinned. "Sometimes. Sometimes I get to come here and drink good coffee and have a break from the noise at home."

Sandy looked at him.

"Boys." He explained. "A house full of boys. And I know, I'm too young. Everyone says it. Started too young, now got four of them and the missus begging for more."

"Wow," Sandy said, raising her eyebrows. She had not pictured DC Sullivan as being a family man, but then, that was probably his intention. To be seen as a professional only, a police officer, not a husband or a father.

"Are we done here?" He asked, his voice low.

She shook her head. "But not even an unreliable witness in this case, eh. Just a motive that points towards Gus Sanders."

"I'll head over in the morning with a search warrant." DC Sullivan said. "Arrest him."

"Do you think he'll confess?" Sandy asked. DC Sullivan looked at her sternly, not prepared to play the game much longer. Sandy wondered if her hunch was wrong, if she had misunderstood.

"I'm confident I'll get the truth out of him." DC Sullivan said. He picked up his coffee cup and moved a step away from the counter.

"Please." Sandy mouthed.

"We're done here." DC Sullivan mouthed back.

Sandy closed her eyes, too anxious to watch her best opportunity slip out of her grasp.

"They doesn't know we did it." The lone customer's voice came from the cafe table at that moment. "They doesn't know we killed him."

DC Sullivan looked at Sandy, his eyes wide in surprise. Sandy nodded and darted out from behind the counter.

Only the click of the cafe door being locked from the inside made the customer look up and see the police officer standing before them.

"You're under arrest for the murder of Dick Jacobs... Ms..." DC Sullivan said, then turned to Sandy for help.

"Ms. Gentry. Cherry Gentry."

16

*S*andy waited in the police station reception area for hours, alternating between pacing anxiously up and down and sitting on the cold hard seat feeling exhausted. Her phone buzzed repeatedly in her pocket, making her guess that the news of the arrest had broken on the news, but she refused to glance at it until she had spoken to DC Sullivan.

He appeared, after 9 pm, looking disheveled and with a dark line of stubble across his jaw.

He gave her a weary smile, held open the door and gestured for her to follow him down the corridor.

She took a seat in his office again and sat awaiting his update.

"Full confession." He said, finally.

"Oh thank goodness," Sandy said, releasing a long breath that she hadn't realised she had been holding.

"It's a sad, sad case." DC Sullivan said. "How did you know she'd out herself?"

"She talks to herself," Sandy said.

"Yeah, I've been in an interview with her for hours, I know that!" DC Sullivan said.

"She doesn't know she's doing it, though. It's like she thinks she's thinking those words, but she says them out loud instead. I just thought if we kept talking about it, and lulled her into that false sense of security, eventually, she'd say - or think - something about it."

"Huh... what made you realise it was her?"

"It was you, really, that comment about it being the perfect crime. And I thought, who could commit the perfect crime? How about someone whos obsessed with reading about them? She can't go a day without a mystery novel, she must know every trick out there for hiding evidence and things. Did she tell you how she did it?"

DC Sullivan nodded. "It's genius, really. She hit him with a frozen salmon. That wouldn't have killed him, I don't think, but it would have blooming hurt, knocked him down, and he hit his head on the pavement, that's what finished it."

"A frozen salmon?" Sandy asked, her eyes wide. "You are kidding?"

"It gets better. She took it home, defrosted it, the cats ate it. No weapon to find, that's why we couldn't find it."

"Wow," Sandy said. "All this because he didn't like her cats?"

"He'd threatened to call the RSPCA and get them removed. She was terrified. I don't think she meant to kill him, if I'm honest. She saw him on her way out of the butcher's, with the fish, and decided to have a chat with him. He wouldn't back down and she just saw red, hit him and panicked."

"So there really weren't any witnesses?" Sandy asked.

DC Sullivan shrugged. "People see things all the time, things they wish they hadn't seen, things they convince themselves they didn't really see. And other times, nobody sees anything at all. Who knows what the truth is here."

Sandy exhaled again. "I'm glad it's over."

"We'll need a statement from you but that can wait until tomorrow." DC Sullivan said.

"Thank you," Sandy said. "Thank you for listening to me, trusting me."

DC Sullivan smiled and shook his head. "Good job she started talking when she did or Gus Sanders would have had a shock in the morning!"

"Oh, crikey, I didn't think about that," Sandy admitted.

"Good night, Sandy." DC Sullivan said.

"Good night, DC Sullivan."

**

Sandy left the police station and instead of turning left back towards Books and Bakes and her car, she crossed the road and walked along Water Lane, taking the next left onto Manor Way. She walked past Cherry's cottage, which was in darkness, and knocked on the vicar's door.

He appeared before her after a few seconds, his easy smile telling her he hadn't heard the news.

"Can I come in?" She asked.

He lead her back into the living room, which was in a similar state of disarray to the last time she had been in there.

"Sit down, Rob." She said. Concern washed over his face and he took a seat.

"They've found the person who killed Dick Jacobs. It was Cherry." Sandy said.

"Ahh." Rob groaned, covering his face with his hands. "Thank you for telling me, Sandy."

Sandy decided not to comment on the lack of surprise in his voice. He was such a calm man, it was impossible to interpret his emotions. "I wondered if you've got a spare key? The cats will need feeding."

"Oh, oh, yes. Good thinking. I do, actually." He said. He stood up and left the room, returning a moment later with a single key on a keyring. "I've never used it before. It feels wrong somehow, to enter a lady's home."

"I can do it?" Sandy offered.

Rob nodded. "Yes. Yes, please. That seems better. Thank you."

Sandy nodded and took the key from his hand, then let herself out of his house and into Cherry's.

She walked past the locked front room door, ignoring the sense of sadness and the unfulfilled possibility that was stored within there, and made tutting noises to attract the cats.

She turned the light on in the hallway, and then the one in the small kitchen. Cats surrounded her. Siamese, tabbies, tortoiseshell, and an enormous black ball of fluff who seemed to eye her with particular understanding.

"Well, guys." She said, ignoring her self-consciousness to treat them the way she thought Cherry would want. It hit her then how foolish Cherry's actions had been. They would cause exactly what she had been trying to avoid happening. "What do you eat when there's no salmon?"

She looked through the cupboards and found an onion, two tins of baked beans and a packet of bourbon biscuits past their use-by date.

"This won't do, will it." She said.

She pulled her phone from her pocket, went to her contacts list and dialled.

"Gus? It's Sandy." She said.

He knocked on the door within ten minutes and held out a carrier bag to her. "I figured someone would ring me tonight."

"You're a star. I know things will change for them soon enough, might as well have one last feast."

"You're a good woman, Sandy," Gus said, unaware that she had been using him as bait earlier that day.

She smiled and closed the door, returning to the cats who swarmed around her feet as they recognised the smell of salmon.

She didn't have the time or skill to defrost and bone a whole salmon, so Gus had prepared one for her and brought over ready to eat fillets.

She placed it on the countertop in the kitchen and sliced the pieces into small chunks, then spread them out amongst the various bowls in the kitchen and back living room. To her surprise, each cat waited by a particular bowl and none attempted to eat until she had finished spreading the food out among all of the bowls.

The large black cat gazed at her.

"OK, you can eat." She said with a laugh. The black cat bent its head and ate.

She shook her head as she pulled her phone out again and made a second call. The black cat watched her. She mouthed 'sorry' to him.

The RSPCA arrived quickly, their knock at the door made Sandy jump.

"We had a tip-off, thought we'd be needed. I was already on the way when your call came in." The short man with huge holes in his earlobes said as he walked in with a cat carrier in each hand. "How many have we got?"

"Erm, I don't know," Sandy admitted. It hadn't occurred to her to count them.

"All right, let's see." The man said. He was a jovial guy, in good spirits to be working so late. Sandy left him to his work, being unfamiliar with cats she could offer little help. Most of the felines walked into a crate when one was placed near them, and Sandy marveled at how well Cherry had trained them.

"It's never normally this easy." The man said as he made another trip out to the van with a crate in each hand. Sandy held the door open for him. "They'll find new homes quick, don't worry."

"Oh, I wasn't," Sandy said. "They're not mine."

The man shrugged, uninterested in the details. He'd realise when he watched the news.

He made quick work of the job, and the cats left the house in silence, only one or two let out a single, restrained meow as they left the house for the last time. Sandy wondered if they'd put up more of a fight over the new cat-food diet they might start the next day. only glancing at him as he carried out pair after pair after pair of cat carriers.

"I think that's it." He said after a final look around the upstairs. He nodded towards the front room. "You're sure there's none in there?"

"No," Sandy said. "There's nobody in there."

"Righteo then. That brings it to twenty-two." He said.

"Wow," Sandy said. "That must be a record?"

The man descended into a deep, belly laugh as he walked down the path towards his van. "Not even close! Not even close!"

Sandy laughed, his happiness infectious. "Well, thank you!"

She closed the door after him and went back into the kitchen, where she washed the cutting board and the knife and tidied them away.

She picked up the single key that hung up on the kitchen rack, and padded down the passage to the front room, which she unlocked and opened with a deep breath. She flicked the light on and stood in the doorway, looking at the perfectly laid table, then moved closer and picked up a knife. The weight of it surprised her. No expense had been spared preparing for the dinner parties that never came.

"What a waste." She whispered, returning the knife to its place. She noticed a slight coat of dust on the plates, fresh dust molecules dropped from the air, and realised that Cherry must have dusted them each day. "What an absolute waste."

With a sigh, she turned off the light and saw herself out of the front room, locking it behind her. She hung the key back up, turned off the kitchen light, then stiffened at a noise.

"Meow." It came again.

She turned to see the large black cat, who had watched her call the RSPCA with such understanding, creep out of the back room.

"Where were you hiding?" She asked, before quickly opening the front door. The man had gone, already on his way to transport the cats to the rescue centre. "Oh no. Well, don't think you're coming home with me. Don't look at me like that!"

**

A few minutes later, she posted the key to Cherry's cottage back through Rob's letterbox. His house was in darkness and she didn't want to disturb him again.

She walked back to her car and opened the passenger door first.

The black cat jumped up onto the passenger seat and curled into a ball.

"One night only, okay?" Sandy said, closing the door and returning back around to the driver's side.

17

*S*andy found an old tin of tuna at the back of her kitchen cupboard and spread it on a small plate for the black cat, who looked at it with disapproval when she set it on the kitchen floor.

"It's the best you'll get in this house," Sandy said, then shook her head at how easily she had become a woman who spoke to animals.

She pulled on her yellow mac, looked back into the kitchen at the cat, who was sitting upright next to the plate of food.

"You can eat." She said, and the cat began to eat. "I'm not saying that to you every day, you know. Not that you're staying, anyway so it doesn't matter."

She shook her head and let herself out of the house. She had shut all of the doors so the cat could only get in the kitchen, where she had left a bowl of water and an old paint tray that she had lined with toilet paper in the hope it would be used as a litter tray.

She drove to the cafe, which was already open and full of people when she parked up outside. As she was about to get out of the car, her phone buzzed. She glanced down at it.

Morning x

She allowed a goofy grin to take over her face, then looked up. Standing outside The Tweed, just a few metres away, and having just watched her receive and grin at his message, was Tom Nelson. She felt her cheeks flush with colour and waved at him, then dived out of the car and straight into the cafe.

"Sandy! Did you hear the news?" Dorie Slaughter called out before the door had even closed after Sandy.

"Yes, Dorie," Sandy said. "I know about Cherry Gentry."

"No! Not that, I mean the news about our new local." Dorie said.

Sandy looked across at her. Sat next to her was Felix, who looked dashing in a three-piece suit. In front of Dorie, was the still wrapped book of poetry that Felix had bought just days earlier.

"Felix?" Sandy asked. "Are you moving in?"

"He's renting my cottage," Dorie explained. "Moving in at the weekend. Things at Elaine's are going so well, no reason we can't make it a more long-term arrangement for me and Jim."

"Oh, fabulous," Sandy said, noting that Elaine wasn't present to agree with Dorie's summary. "Well, Felix, you'll be made very welcome here. I hope to see your face often for a coffee or a browse around the books."

"A coffee and a cake." Coral corrected, ever the saleswoman.

Sandy laughed. "A coffee and a cake, then."

The door opened then and DC Sullivan walked in, scanned the faces until he met Sandy's, and walked across to her. "I'm heading back to the city now, these guys can finish up the loose ends. I just wanted to say goodbye... until the next time, I guess."

"Oh!" Sandy exclaimed. "I'm sure there won't be a next time. We've got to be done with our bad luck, I reckon."

"We'll see." DC Sullivan shrugged, then gave a general wave to the cafe and left.

"He's growing on me, that man," Coral said.

"Calm down, he's married!" Sandy scolded.

Coral shrugged. "I just mean he's very pleasant."

"Yeah right," Sandy said with a laugh.

"What are your plans tonight, then, fancy popcorn and a chick flick with me?"

Sandy tried to hide the horror on her face as she remembered what day it was.

"I'm joking, don't worry!" Coral laughed. "I'm guessing you've got a hot date?"

"Erm... I think I might have?" Sandy said. Tom had messaged her to say he would pick her up at 7 pm. She had a fluttering in her stomach when she thought about the explanation he was going to offer for his odd behaviour. Surely he wouldn't be insensitive enough to take her out on Valentine's Day to tell her whatever they'd had between them was over? She couldn't stand to think about it.

**

She was ready twenty minutes before Tom was due to arrive.

He hadn't given her any idea on how to dress, so she had spent an hour trying on various combinations of clothes creating a range of casual and formal looks. In the end, she had chosen a glittery silver dress with long sleeves. It came down to her knees and showed just a suggestion of cleavage. It was one of the pieces in her wardrobe that she felt most confident and comfortable in.

Her plan was to hide out in her bedroom and watch Tom arrive. If he was dressed more casual than she was, she had a reserve outfit of dark blue jeans and a cashmere sweater laid out on her bed.

And so, on Valentine's evening, she found herself sat on her bed in the dark, listening out for the sound of a car approaching, while the black cat sat on the floor watching her. Her make-up was heavier than normal, meaning she had used eyeliner and a little bronzer as well as foundation and mascara. Her hair was loose and straight, and every few minutes she left her bedroom to go to the bathroom and examine it as she was convinced it looked too flat.

It was on one of those trips to the bathroom that she must have missed the car approach, pull up, and stop.

She was attempting to push more body into her hair when a knock came from downstairs.

"Oh, no." She cursed. She dived into her bedroom and peered out through the window, but the front door was covered by a small ledge, and she couldn't see anything more than the end of a man's leg and what looked in the dark to be a smart shoe.

She took a deep breath and descended the stairs, then opened the door and flashed a smile at Tom.

She felt breathless at the sight of him, in a grey suit, with a bunch of lilies clutched in front of him.

He looked stunned at her appearance.

"Sandy... you look incredible." He said. He held the flowers out to her. "I know everyone gets roses on Valentine's Day, but that seemed a bit too predictable."

"I haven't got you anything." She admitted. "I was a little

nervous you might take me out to tell me were just friends, or something. Ew, I shouldn't have said that, sorry, forget I said it."

"Sandy, I don't want to be just friends," Tom said. "Trust me."

She smiled and followed him out of the house. He held open the passenger door for her and closed it once she was sat down, then got in the driver's side and turned on the engine.

They drove through to the next village in a comfortable silence. Sandy wanted him to lead the conversation when he was ready, even though she was desperate to ask him to explain himself.

They pulled up outside a red brick building, a restaurant that Sandy had heard of but never been to before. A valet took the keys from Tom and he held out his hand, which she took in hers. They walked into the grand building hand in hand, and Sandy tried to remember as much about the feeling, and the experience, as possible.

She knew that Coral and Cass would grill her for details when they arrived to take her breakfast the next morning, an invitation that she knew had been offered so they could hear how the night had gone.

"This is amazing." She whispered to Tom as the head waiter lead them into a grand dining room. Their table was small, but they were right at the far end of the room, meaning they had privacy from the other diners. Sandy's foot brushed against Tom's leg underneath the table and he blushed.

"I'd recommend the duck to begin," Tom said, then groaned. "Sorry, that sounded like I'm here all the time. I've never been before, but I read a review in the newspaper last week and it said the duck to start, the risotto for main and the cheese board for dessert. Right, hopefully, that's the awkwardness out of the way."

"Tom, just relax. It's only me." Sandy said.

"That's just it, it's you. You make me nervous." Tom admitted.

Sandy felt her cheeks flush. Terror-inducing was hardly a good effect to have on a potential suitor.

"Shall I just try and explain what's been happening?" He asked.

"I think you should."

"Ok... well... I may look like a grown man, I may even sound like one occasionally, but I think in reality I'm still a young kid and when I get scared, I bury my head in the sand. I've always done it, when I was flunking maths, I didn't ask for help or anything, just stopped revising, pretended everything was OK and failed the exam. And I've never learned the lesson. And that's what this has been. I know I went a bit cold on you, stopped texting and stuff. And then I saw you, and you were just fine, you were laughing and you seemed happy, so I thought you'd not even noticed. You know?"

"Because I have so many dashing men sending me texts, you mean?" Sandy teased, but Tom didn't laugh.

"You could do for all I know." He said. "You're beautiful, Sandy. You're absolutely beautiful and you say things that I'm thinking, it's like there's so much we've got in common. I got scared. I got scared of this."

"This? Dinner out in a lovely restaurant?" Sandy asked. She was being facetious, she knew, but she hadn't expected such emotion from Tom and she was unsure how else to react.

"I'm in love with you, Sandy, that's what scared me," Tom said.

Sandy gulped and searched for the right words.

"It's okay, I said I'd explain tonight, I didn't say I'd put you on the spot and ask for anything from you. I love you, and I think you should know, even though it's terrifying me to admit this. I've never felt like this before and I guess I had to hide for a bit and get my head around it. I'm sorry."

Sandy reached across the table and took Tom's hand in hers. "I love you too."

"What?" He asked.

She nodded. "I realised this week, although Coral told me she knew before I did. She knows everything before I do."

"Wow... does this mean..."

Sandy laughed at his nerves.

"Does this mean we're a couple? I mean, I guess the question is, will you be my girlfriend? God, that sounds awful at my age."

"Yes, I'll be your girlfriend, Tom Nelson. Or your woman friend, however you want to describe it." Sandy agreed.

Tom squeezed her hand and reached across the table, planting a delicate kiss on her lips.

"I've got something to ask you in return," Sandy said on a whim.

Tom looked at her, his gaze curious now, nerves faded away.

"Do you fancy a trip to Scotland?"

BANANA CREAM PIE TO DIE FOR

Ingredients:

1 cup sugar
   1/4 cup corn flour
   1/2 teaspoon salt
   3 cups skimmed milk
   2 large eggs, beaten
   3 tablespoons butter
   1 1/2 teaspoons vanilla extract
   1 pastry case (9 inches), baked
   2 large firm bananas
   1 cup whipped cream
   1 teaspoon cinnamon

Method:

1. In a large saucepan, combine the sugar, corn flour, salt and milk and mix until smooth.

2. Cook and stir over a medium-heat until the mixture thickens and becomes bubbly.

3. Reduce heat; cook and stir for 2 more minutes.

4. Remove from heat. Stir a small amount of the hot filling into the eggs, then return all to the pan.

5. Return mixture to heat and bring to a gentle boil. Cook and stir for 2 more minutes.

6. Remove from heat. Gently stir in butter and vanilla. Transfer into a bowl and cover with cling film.

7. Place in fridge for 30 minutes.

8. Spread half of the custard mix into pastry case. Slice bananas and arrange over the filling.

9. Pour remaining custard mix over bananas. Spread with whipped cream. Dust cinnamon over whipped cream.

10. Refrigerate for 6 hours or overnight.

11. Enjoy!

THANK YOU FOR READING

As an independent author, my success depends on readers sharing the word about my books and leaving honest reviews online.

If you enjoyed this book, please consider leaving an honest review on Amazon or GoodReads.

I know that your time is precious, and I am grateful that you chose to spend some of your time entering the world of Waterfell Tweed with me.

To see the the latest releases, visit:

http://monamarple.com/the-series/

And to receive exclusive content and the latest news, join my VIP Reader List by visiting:

http://monamarple.com/vip-reader-list/

ABOUT THE AUTHOR

Mona Marple is a mother, author and coffee enthusiast.

When she isn't busy writing a cozy mystery, she's probably curled up somewhere warm reading one.

She lives in the beautiful Peak District (where Waterfall Tweed is set in her imagination!) with her husband and daughter.

ALSO BY MONA MARPLE

Once Upon a Crime (Waterfell Tweed Cozy Mystery Series:
Book One)

A Tale of Two Bodies (Waterfell Tweed Cozy Mystery Series:
Book Two)

Printed in Great Britain
by Amazon